Zimbolicious 10th Anniversary:

New and Collected Fictions

Edited by Tendai Rinos Mwanaka

Mwanaka Media and Publishing Pvt Ltd,
Chitungwiza Zimbabwe
*
Creativity, Wisdom and Beauty

Publisher: *Mmap*
Mwanaka Media and Publishing Pvt Ltd
24 Svosve Road, Zengeza 1
Chitungwiza Zimbabwe
mwanaka@yahoo.com
mwanaka13@gmail.com
www.africanbookscollective.com/publishers/mwanaka-media-and-publishing
https://facebook.com/MwanakaMediaAndPublishing/

Distributed in and outside N. America by African Books Collective
orders@africanbookscollective.com
www.africanbookscollective.com

ISBN: 978-1-77928-204-0
EAN: 9781779282040

DISCLAIMER
All views expressed in this publication are those of the author and do
not necessarily reflect the views of *Mmap*.

TABLE OF CONTENTS

About editor

Tendai Rinos Mwanaka is a multidisciplinary artist, writer, musician, editor, publisher and producer with over 70 individual books and curated anthologies published in US, Northern Ireland, UK, Cameroon and Zimbabwe. He has 5 music albums, with new album, *For Mberikwazvo: The Winter After* (2025) recently released and his music is playing in at least 18 radio stations in US, Canada, UK, France, Israel, Brazil and Australia. He has hundreds of paintings and drawings, thousands of photographs, some exhibited, published and sold. His pieces have appeared in over 500 journals in over 35 countries and his books and writing is translated into at least 11 languages. His music can be licensed here: https://www.songtradr.com/tendai.mwanaka. And find him here: https://m.facebook.com/tendai.mwanaka

Contributors Bio Notes

Matthew Kunashe Chikono is an editor and short story writer from Chitungwiza, Zimbabwe. He has complied and edited *Prima Anthology* and *The Rules of the City*. He also co-edited *Zimbolicious Volume 8*. He has published two solo short story collections *Dreams of Paradise* and *Blue Threads and other stories* with the third *Shreds* to be released in 2026. facebook.com/passionatewriterspen

    Mildred Mutize, born on 20 April 1983, is a Zimbabwean fiction writer and motivational speaker. Born and raised in Harare, her passion for writing sprouted in her early childhood days and later blossomed during High School where she scooped a number of literature awards. She has authored several short stories which are all hinged on suspense, mystery and thrill. She is married and has three children.

    I'm **Tanea Nyika**, an 18-year-old female high school student from Zimbabwe with a remarkable talent and creativity when it comes to writing and storytelling. Despite juggling my academic pursuits, I have already achieved the extraordinary feat of publishing three novels by the age of 17 among which one is a poetry anthology, *Scarred Words*. My personal literary prowess and dedication to my craft have garnered attention both locally and internationally. As I prepare to graduate this year, the world eagerly anticipates the next captivating book in my burgeoning writing career.

    Oscar Gwiriri is a Zimbabwean published in more than 60 books, both fiction and text books. His two books *Hatiponi* and *Chitima nditakure* were NAMA awards nominees in 2019. He is a Certified Forensic Investigations Professional (CFIP) and a Certified Information Systems Security Professional (CISSP). He also holds a *Master of Science in Strategic Management Degree,* *Bachelor of Business Administration, Associates of Arts in Business Administration, Diploma in Logistics and Transport (CILT, UK), Diploma in Workplace Safety and Health, Commanding United Nations Peacekeeping Operations Certificate*, and many other professional qualifications. He likes writing in his vernacular language (Shona) most.

David Chasumba is a Zimbabwean Writer and Poet. He has published two short story collections with Carnelian Heart Publishing: 2023 NAMA award winning, *The Mad Man on First Street and Other Short Stories (2022)* and *Behind the Façade and Other Stories (2024)*. David's poems have been published by Kalahari Review, Ipikai Poetry Journal, British Haiku Society anthology (2023), in *Best "New" African Poets (2023)* anthology and in *MEN: An International Anthology of African and Latin American Writers, Volume 3*. David lives in Bexhill-on sea, East Sussex, UK. X: @davidchasumba22

I am **Sheila Banda**. A wife and mother to two boys. I am a librarian at National Free Library in Bulawayo. Currently staying in Bulawayo and studying towards a degree in Library and Information science. Passionate about writing, my icon being Tsitsi Dangarembga.

Yeukai 'Mimyie' Benhura is an aspirant writer from Zimbabwe. Her favoured themes are family and women empowerment. She is a member of Zimbabwe Women Writers and Poetritis Nirvana organizations that work to empower writers.

Phumulani Chipandambira is a freelance writer who lives in Norton, Zimbabwe. He likes reading and writing short stories and poems. His works have been published in various local magazines, blogs and newspapers.

Hosea Tokwe is a Chief Library Assistant at Midlands State University in Gweru. His first short story appeared in the *Munyori Journal*. He has other works published in *Zimbolicious Volume 1* and *Best New African Poets*. Other short stories have also appeared in *The Mosi-Au-Tunya Literary Journal* and the Artmosterrific Magazine.

Nicole Kazembe is a twenty-seven year old female, avid although inexpert poetry and short story writer with a published poetry book titled *Catching feelings*, which is available on Amazon. When not writing, she enjoys reading and procrastinating while watching television. She is currently working on a short story book

Dumisani Charles Kufaruwenga was born in Chivi, Kufaruwenga Village near Tongogara Growth Point in Shurugwi Communal Lands. Both his parents were teachers. He completed "A" Level at Fletcher High School in Gweru and thereafter graduated with a law degree from University of Zimbabwe. Dumisani Kufaruwenga is currently practicing law in Harare

Christopher 'Voice' Kudyahakudadirwe is a Zimbabwean freelance writer, photographer, poet and teacher living and working in South Africa. He recently published a collection of short stories entitled *The Big Noise and Other Noises*. His poems have been published in an anthology entitled *Harvest: The University of the Western Cape Masters in Creative Writing Poetry Anthology 2016* and on his poetry blog: https://kudyahakudadirwe.wordpress.com/. He holds a Masters in Creative Writing from the University of the Western Cape. He is currently in the process of enrolling for a PhD in Creative Writing.

Takunda Shepherd Chikomo is a Zimbabwean author based in Chitungwiza. With three books to his name, "Curtains an anthology of poems", "These things also happened to me" and his latest book "Deflowered", he is one of the most promising writers to emerge out of Zimbabwe and he has just begun!

Preface

10 years ago we started on the Zimbolicious Journey by issuing out *Zimbolicious Anthology Vol 1*, which was an anthology of Zimbabwean poets. The Vol 2 was still a focus on Zimbabwean poets, but in the third volume we expanded it to embrace other Zimbabwean arts and literature, e.g. drawings, paintings, essays, short stories etc.., and ever since this anthology series has been publishing all these until the last we issued, Vol 9. So we have decided this year to look back and ahead this journey by issuing out anniversary anthologies. Because in the fifth volume we focussed on an anniversary centred on the genre we started with, poetry, we have decided the 10th year anniversary should focus on prose (fiction and Nonfiction), thus we created two anniversary anthologies. One for fiction, one for nonfiction. We collected some of the essays and stories and added a few new ones from contributors of these anthologies

This one, *Zimbolicious 10th Anniversary Anthology: New and Collected Fictions* has 27 fiction pieces. Fiction that deals with a gamut of Zimbabwean stories. Chikono starts the anthology with his newest fiction piece and drives the anthology forward with a total of 7 pieces. He has been our biggest fiction contributor over the years. Others like Kudyahakudadirwe, Tokwe, Gwiriri aren't far behind. We have stories to do with the politics of Zimbabwe, death, paranormal, science fiction, relationships, cancer, motherhood, religion, young children stories, a slice of the bus journey from Harare to Chitungwiza which is one of the most influential places in Zimbabwe, service delivery, unemployment of graduates etc... Each story is imbued with that typical dry wit sarcasm of Zimbabweans, and the beauty of an artful country and culture that our country is known for. Enjoy!

Lone wolf long wound

Matthew Kunashe Chikono

He had started having nightmares again. It was different this time though; instead of waking up with sheets drenched in sweat and pillows soaked in tears, it was his pyjama's shorts that would be stained and sticky with sponge. During those unconscious episodes, Felix had one too many times tried to escape her grip and flee out of her reach, but the girl with her seductive ways had made him come to her over and over again.

Felix opened his eyes and waited for the shame of what he had done in his sleep wash over him. It didn't take long; he could feel the huge bed he had slept alone in widening and himself shrinking on the middle. Felix cussed the hotel staff for putting such a big bed in his room; it was big enough for him and two call girls. He brushed the thought aside; the bed was big enough for him and his wife.

His wife!

He had already forgotten about her. Felix quickly jumped out of bed and ran into the shower. Few minutes later he was done and well dressed. He called the front desk and told them to make his car ready.

"Do you want any breakfast sir?" The girl on the receiver asked.

"No, I am late. Thanks Natalie." Felix said. He was impressed by the girl's timidness during those awkward phone calls. Felix Nhanga had taken the girl up to his room few weeks earlier. When the girl tried to come up again, she found out she had already been replaced with another girl from the staff. Every now and then when they crossed path in the reception area, Natalie always kept on her unwavering professional straight face. Felix had told the girl that he could do whatever he wanted, he was a director after all!

"Mr. Director sir," the girl's voice came through the phone few minutes later, "the car is ready for you."

Felix Nhanga dashed down from the two-story building to his car. He didn't want to be seen by any of the other guests of the place or be seen by the staff. He quickly dismissed the driver and drove himself away from the dirty building that he had been sleeping in for months. He had to go home to his wife and children who missed him dearly.

Felix had not thought through this journey back home; he had failed to consider the traffic congestion that always occurred in the CBD every Saturday morning. The streets of Harare were jammed with Japanese cars and street vendors who burrowed any space that wasn't filled with garbage. Felix quickly rolled up the window of his car before the stench of rotting cabbages and unwashed bodies could suffocate him.

Half an hour later, Felix was still a couple of hundred metres from the hotel. He was already regretting his decision of using his own car instead of the government issued Benz, which had sirens and flashing lights that would have cleared the road for him. He had been sitting in the car for a long time that he started wondering if going home was a good idea. Being stuck in the traffic was definitely a sign from the universe telling him not to go to his wife. He chose to listen to the universe.

Felix made an illegal turn in his SUV and made his way to his offices. It was a Saturday and it would be empty. He would take some time to calm down in the parking lot before trying to go home again. When he arrived at the tall white building, he found the parking lot almost empty. He didn't even bother to park at his reserved spot. The clock on the dashboard read 8.05 am.

It was quiet. Felix Nhanga closed his eyes a bit, waiting to be rejuvenated and continue his way back to his family. His mind went back to the nightmare he had had. There was a girl in it. Her face was distorted, he knew why. She wasn't just a random girl his mind had conjured up to please his immoderate libido, no, she was a relic from his own past. His first true love, if his memories could be trusted. He couldn't trust his memories, not after betraying him by forgetting her face.

For twenty years Felix had never thought of her, now it was all he could dream of. Twenty years; surely, she was no longer the naive, energetic teenage girl Felix barely remembered. Back in the village he would call her and they would be sneaking about in the maize fields or cattle kraals. Felix was still a herd boy taking care of the girl's father's cattle. He hadn't done well in his examinations and was waiting for a miracle in order to escape the mundane village life.

As much as he tried, Felix could neither recall her face nor her name but what he remembered was the first time he had taken her. It was behind her father's kraal where a cow was about to birth a calf. Her father had just left to call the vet nurse who lived few houses away. By the time he was back, the deed had already been done. Sitting in his car seat Felix started getting aroused as he remembered the adrenaline and excitement of the thought of being caught combined with the pleasure of coitus.

A rude knock on the window stopped him from spunking. Felix quickly rolled down the window to a face of a light skinned older man peering through.

"Morning boss." The man said with a grin.

"Why were you peering in to my car?" Felix asked, "Did you see anything?"

"No boss," the man continued grinning, "The glass is tinted."

"Yes, it is." Felix said as relief washed over his face. His car, just like hundreds bought from the overseas, had tinted windows. The man tried to sell cellphone chargers to him but Felix wasn't interested. The man ran away when Felix threatened to shoot him with a non-existent gun.

With the distraction gone, Felix decided to continue his daydreaming about his nameless first love. What he remembered vividly was the sex. After the first time behind the kraal, where the girl had bled, cried and threatened not to see him anymore, they did it a dozen times more; in his hut, behind her mother's kitchen, at the riverbank, and one time he dare to make her skip school and they did it on her father's bed.

During one of those encounters, he asked her what she would do if she were to get pregnant from all the copulation they were having.

"I would marry the boy next door whilst I wait for you to come back to take me." She replied.

"And the baby?"

"It would be a she. I would call her Eustancia and tell her stories about his father who went to the city to make money." She had slyly smiled.

The conversation was imprinted in his brain. Few weeks later he left the village for the city. He told the girl he would come back for her in a few months. He was going to whisky her away to a happy place. That had been twenty years earlier. The nameless girl was now a woman, probably married and with children of her own.

The thought that he might have left a girl pregnant with his child made Felix change his way when he came to the city. He now used protection. For the women he had retained for the long hull, he offered money for abortion. Felix believed that it wouldn't be prudent for the streets of Harare to be filled with his bastard children. One bastard was enough, if the girl in the village had ever got pregnant.

The memory of the girl from the village stayed with him. Even as he slept with other women, it was the thought of her that made him release. Her memory tainted his mind the first couple of months he had come to the city.

Felix Nhanga slapped himself and come back to his senses. He slapped his cheek again for thinking about a mirage instead of his wife who sat with his five children waiting for him to come home. The five rats were noisy and never gave him a moment to relax but his wife was a saint.

Felix had scored her the first month he arrived in the city. She was an only daughter of a permanent minister in agriculture. She had just come back from the Americas where a white boy had broken her heart. In order to mend it, she had shut herself at her father's mansion where Felix was the garden boy maintaining the grass and flowers. After lunch Felix would stop his work and watch her swim in her bikini. He was smitten.

A year later she had charmed her father to allow her to marry Felix in a private ceremony. At first, her father had protested because of the age gap, Felix being nine years younger, but few weeks before the wedding Felix found himself as a senior manager in an agricultural parastatal under his to be father-in-law's ministry. Eighteen years later, with five children in tow, Felix was now the Managing Director, reporting only to the minister of agriculture himself. The only paper he had used to rise the ranks was a marriage certificate.

With the realisation that his life, without his wife, was nothing Felix put the car in reverse and negotiated his way out of the car park. He pointed the bonnet towards the direction his wife was and started driving like the rest of the maniacs in the road.

Then he saw her, the girl from his nightmares, standing next to a defunct traffic light. She had one shoe on and another in her hand. A

13

look of bewilderment on her face. His brain screamed eureka; that was the face the tides of time had washed away from the shores of his mind. It didn't make sense to Felix, the girl on the street was about twenty years younger than his first true love.

Felix hit the brakes and his car skidded to a stop. He felt the bump and knew another car had hit his in the rear. He didn't get out of the car; he was at fault here. He kept staring at the girl.

"Hello Miss!" He shouted through the window, "Are you lost? Can I help you?"

The girl looked at him; she saw nothing, her mind trapped in the realm of its own, unable to fathom what was happening around her.

"Look, I am from the government." Felix said waving his medical aid card," I can help you. Just get into the car before you get arrested."

The mentioning of getting arrested jousted the girl back to the living. She quickly scrambled into the car without saying any word. Felix slammed the accelerator before the cars behind him started blaring their horns. He hit a porthole in the middle of the road. He could see the girl, with the corner of his eye, fumbling with the seatbelt. She gave up after the third attempt.

"What happened?"

"I got robbed in the street." The girl started, "They took my bag and money."

"Are you hurt anywhere?" Felix asked.

"No, they just grabbed the bag and ran. No one helped. They got my money and my address book, now don't know what to do." The girl was near tears.

"Shame, people here don't help," Felix continued, "listen I can help you with bus fare. Where are you going?"

"I don't know where I am going," the girl couldn't help with the tears," You see I am looking for someone. His address and phone number were in the book that got stolen with my things. Even if you lend me money, I wouldn't know where to go."

"It's okay, one thing at a time. I am not lending you the money; I am giving it to you for free. I don't have it now, it's in the hotel room near here. Is it okay if we go there now and pick it up?" He asked. The girl did not answer. She started to pull down her skirt to cover her bare knees.

The rest of the short journey to the hotel was filled with silence. The girl stared out of the window, away from her knight in shining armor. It wasn't what Felix had in mind.

By the way, what is your name?" Felix realised bit later that he had forgotten to ask.

"Eustancia," the girl replied," Eustancia Gwanza."

Felix's heart skipped a bit and he nearly hit a beggar sitting along the road. He looked at the girl. He could imagine his mouth saying what a coincidence it was; that he might have a daughter with the same name but he wasn't sure if the daughter existed. He wasn't sure if the supposed daughter was even a daughter, maybe it was a son. Or maybe the mother of the daughter had gone with another name. Worse maybe the daughter was never born because the pregnancy never came to term. Also, maybe it was just a pregnant scare so he might not have a daughter with the same name after all. Felix envisioned the girl calling him a delinquent before tossing herself out of the moving car.

"Eustancia, that's a nice name. We have arrived at the hotel," the Director said, "Can you please come up with me for a moment please?"

The girl followed closely behind him, her eyes on the ground. He held his head high; he wanted Natalie to see his newest conquest. He glanced at her desk as he entered the hotel lobby. Natalie was busy looking under her desk, pretending not to see him. He hoped she was jealous. He went upstairs to his room before the news of his new conquest had spread among the hotel staff.

The girl needed much coercion to accept the invitation to sit on the bed. She sat with her hands on her lap, admiring her fingernails whilst waiting for the gift of bus fare promised. Felix started rack sacking through drawers and cardboards.

"Where did I put it?" Felix murmured under his breath. He checked his pockets from the previous day's trousers, he was sure he still had one condom left. The condom was not anywhere to be seen.

He couldn't hold it any longer. He unzipped his trousers and walked over to the bed. The girl stared at it. He pushed her until she lay with her back on the bed. Felix didn't meet any resistance as he scuffled with her clothes. She didn't struggle or utter a sound as Felix mounted her and he was done few minutes later.

A while later they were on the hotel lobby on their way to the car. The lobby was filled with the hotel staff busy doing nothing. Felix glanced at the reception desk, Natalie wasn't there, and he hoped she had gone to the bathroom to cry.

The girl got into the car without a word, she managed to put on the seatbelt in the first attempt. Felix unable to make sense of the silence, pulled out a bundle two-dollar notes and handed it to her. Felix figured it would be enough for bus fare and the remainder to buy a pill if it ever came to that. The Director put the car in gear and started driving towards the nearest bus stop.

They arrived at the bus terminus. Felix nudged the girl to leave his car. The girl got out without protest. Before she closed the door, Felix thought he saw a tear dropping from her eye, but he wasn't sure. The girl stood amongst the masses not sure where to go next. That wasn't his problem anymore.

Felix Nhanga looked at the girl one last time. He wondered if she was the daughter of the woman from his nightmares she had borne for him. No, that happened only in Nigerian movies and Netflix shows. Besides, Felix thought, his life wasn't a contemporary fictional story were such coincidence happened. His life was real and it demanded him to do something; drive out of the city to where his wife and five children waited for him to come home.

The end

The Deformed Dream

Christopher Kudyahakudadirwe

For a whole week now, you have been all over, everywhere in the big city chasing after one of the two million phantom jobs that your president promised in the last elections. You had voted for him hopefully because you were dreaming of a good job after university especially after your widowed mother had literally closed her livestock pens in order for you to get the BSc degree that hangs proudly on the wall in your mother's sitting room. You had believed him without doubt that things were going to be on the mend and the economy would flourish birthing the jobs that would, perhaps, help to reopen the livestock pens of your mother. Disappointingly, three years into the five-year term of the old president, no jobs have been created for the millions of youths who are leaving school. Your anger and frustration boils inside you like a tropical volcano which would erupt any time as you trudge the potholed streets of the capital city.

On Monday, you had been to the light industry, just across the heavily polluted river, where you had heard over the weekend that a Chinese company was recruiting people to pack plastic toys that they were manufacturing. For four hours, you had waited outside the gate amongst the growing number of job-seekers only to be told by this fat, balding Chinese man that they wanted those with a BSc degree for the ten vacancies that were available. And you had forgotten your degree certificate at home. So, you were just like the others who had no education at all. You slouched away like a hyena whose kill has been taken over by a very hungry pride of lions.

Then on Tuesday you woke up before the sun showed above the eastern horizon and arrived at the site where the American Embassy was constructing its new headquarters in the city. The contracted company wanted 'daga-boys' and you had remembered to take with you your BSc degree certificate just in case they wanted degreed 'daga-boys'. To your disappointment, the interview required that an applicant should be able to throw a brick high up to the second floor of the building. Your efforts, unfortunately, could not send a standard brick further than the first floor. It was a very disgraceful day especially when other young men like you were able to do with ease what you had failed to do.

Wednesday: another unfortunate day. A fertilizer company in the heavy industrial area wanted people to off-load a whole train that had hurled two hundred tonnes of fertilizer from the seaport into the country. These were 50kg net bags and you are only 47kg with your clothes and shoes on.

"You'll be paid according to the number of bags you will off-load," the foreman announced as soon as you were engaged. "This means you'll stack your bags in one stack and at the end of the day we'll count them. The more you off-load the more you earn. It's 50cents a bag."

No one was turned away. It was half past seven in the morning. There were men and women who had answered to the call for the job. The fifty-odd of you who had gathered for the job earnestly attacked the train like ants attacking the carcass of a dead python. The employer had assigned his permanent workers to climb into the wagons so that they would load the bags onto your heads and you would then carry them into the warehouse. So, when the first 50kg bag of urea landed on your dread-locked head, your knees buckled under you and before the bag crushed you under, you let fall on the platform and its powdery contents were all over.

"You're fired, boy! This work is for men," the foreman was fuming as he shooed you out of the warehouse yard.

And that was the end of your job. All the castles you had built came crumbling on you like the bag of urea.

The previous day, Thursday, you spent it in First Street playing street soccer with other university graduates. The *WhatsApp* group message had requested you to come dressed in your graduation gown complete with the mortar-board, hood and rolled up papers to represent the certificates. The occasion was meant to be a statement-making get together to protest the president's failure to create the 2.2million jobs promised in the run-up to the 2013 elections. In attendance, the message said, would be the riot police, not those who quell riots, but those who facilitate it to happen (according to the term commonly used); the street vendors and those queueing for their money at the banking halls in First Street. So, you had cordoned off the area between HM Barbours and Ok Stores for the stadium. By eight o'clock, the place was bristling with the police in their egg-heads, brandishing glass shields and batons that quivered like the spines of agitated hedgehogs. The game was played and the media had a field day. The following day the police where blamed by the politicians for allowing you to denigrate the name of the president like that. Your story was the subject of a heated debate in the parliament between the ruling party and opposition party members of parliament.

Today is Friday. Some call it *Faraiday* – a day to be happy. It is the end of the week and people celebrate it in many ways possible. Those with extra money to spend go to the taverns and beerhalls to drown their financial problems with liquor and others go for *gochi-gochi* to kill their craving for grilled meat. These celebrations require financing. So, on Thursday evening when you heard about the grave digging jobs that had been created at Mbudzi Cemetery by an undertaking company, you were there before the sun licked the eastern horizon of the city.

"We want people who can dig at least three graves a day," the pot-bellied prospective employer bellows after several picks and shovels have been off-loaded from the white truck that immediately drives off.

There is a scramble for the tools. In this disorganised melee you manage to grab a pick and a shovel. The rule here, as you learnt later, is that those who have not been able to lay their hands on a tool have not been hired. You are happy to have secured a pick and a shovel. Those who would have managed a pick or a shovel only have to work together and that meant splitting the pay at the end of the day. While waiting for the truck to arrive word had circulated saying that the employer only paid those who would have dug three graves per day.

That way he was assured of finished graves since it was weekend, a time when most burials in the city were conducted.

Mr Pot Belly shows you where your work starts and ends. Soon sods of newly dug, sweet smelling soil are flying out and forming small hills next to the deepening rectangular holes you are digging. Diggers are getting shorter and shorter as the holes deepen. Shirts have been taken off and are flapping on the handles of the picks or the shovels depending on which tool is in use at any given time. The whole area looks like a sweet potato field where moles are busy burrowing and creating mounds of soil everywhere. This is work for a man and a half and not for those who attended school at St George's or Peter House.

By the time you are waist deep callouses have popped up in your hands; your back is aching and your throat is as dry as a desert; you cannot swallow any saliva because there is none to swallow. When you stop to take a rest, a lot of thoughts flash through your mind. You remember when you were at St George's doing your fourth-year secondary school. You were a brilliant and eloquent student to the extent that your English language teacher had drafted you into the debate club which was mainly an Upper 6 elite club. You were so good at presenting your argument such that you became the opening speaker all the time you went for a debating competition. When you were in the Lower 6 you went overseas where you became the darling of audiences by beating the native speakers of the language. But then that was before your father's empire crumbled and he later died of stress resulting in your mother as well as you going to live in the rural areas

That was then and now after university you are facing the reality of your run-down country.

As the sun creeps to the zenith, you have not finished digging the first grave. Some of your fellow diggers are doing their second hole and others are starting on their third. Your hands are on fire. You dig for three minutes and take a rest of five. It would seem like you are not going to finish this one grave. The pain in your hands is very unbearable. You cannot bend your fingers to hold the handle of the pick anymore. *But I'm an educated man, why should I suffer this way just like those who have not been to school,* you ask yourself. Then what is the purpose of going to school if one has to do the work that an uneducated person can do? Who should answer that? You shake your head slowly as you contemplate whether to carry on working or quit at that moment.

The urge to quit overruns the one to keep digging. So, without telling Mr Pot Belly or anyone for that matter, you scramble out of the grave and you put on your shirt and head towards your aunt's house in the western part of the city. Two syllable words are spewing from your mouth as you walk away from the cemetery. You are cursing the day you were born: you are cursing the president of the country accusing him of blatant lying; you are so frustrated that you kick the stones out of your way. You blame the ruling party which created the situation that caused your father's companies to go under. You are so angry that you do not notice the shiny piece of metal that is revealed when you kick a stone out of your way until you are three strides away. Something tells you to go back and check what it is that is shining like that.

It is a folded $1 bond coin!

You pick up the deformed coin and brush off the little sand that clings to it. What could have folded the coin to be folded like that, you wonder silently? You look at it carefully. No crack on it, right. Now many other things are crowding your muddled mind. It is Friday. A day when people celebrate the end of the week. At least I've somewhere to start from, you say to yourself as you quicken your steps towards the nearest bar. A $1 bond coin can buy you four litres of opaque beer. You are now feeling like a human being. Your gaiety is that of someone who has command of his destiny. The power of money! Isn't it the reason why people wake up early each day and run away from their warm and comfortable beds to look for, you muse as you enter the beerhall.

The noise in the beerhall does not reduce you to a beggar begging for masese from those who have the money to buy it. With exaggerated confidence, you walk straight to the barman.

"Barman, a two-litre pack of Super, please!" you proffer the folded $1 bond coin. You throat is already pumping like that of an angry frog.

The barman takes the deformed coin and looks at it.

"Sorry, we don't accept that kind of money." He literally throws it at you.

"But it's money, isn't it?"

"Not in this bar," the barman says as he goes to serve the next waiting customer.

All hope is gone. You pick up the deformed coin and go to sit at a table right in the darkest corner of the beerhall. You are afraid that he might think of calling the police and having you arrested for trying to defraud the beerhall. Alone in that dark corner, you listen to your hands throbbing and your back crack-aching and thinking: had the barman allowed you to buy with that deformed coin you would be wetting your throat with the thick Super which many people had christened: food and drink.

Then an idea dawns in your mind. You jump to your feet and quickly get out of the beerhall. Your legs take you towards the shops and surely there under the veranda, surrounded by boxes and boxes full of old broken shoes is the cobbler. He is busy applying glue to the sole of a shoe that he is repairing. The smell of glue is thick in the air around him.

"Excuse me, sir!"

The man looks up and then back at his handwork. "What is it, my son?"

"Can I use your hammer?"

"For what?"

You put your hand in your back pocket searching for the folded $1 bond coin. It is not there in that pocket. You check in the other and your hand comes out with it.

"I want to straighten this. The barman wouldn't take it like this."

The man continues applying glue to the sole of the shoe and you can see he has agreed to helping you. Then when he finishes what he is doing he stretches out his hand and you hand him the coin. He takes out his hammer and the cobbler anvil on which he puts the deformed coin. With two well directed strokes the coin is as good as new.

"Thank you very much," you say as you stretch your hand to receive the mended coin.

"Not before you have paid me." His whiskers are twitching like those of a cat that is preparing to eat a mouse it has just killed.

"How much?" you are calculating that if need be you will give him fifty cents and then you take the remainder to the barman and get yourself at least two litres of Super.

"One dollar fifty."

"Just for what you've done?"

"My charges start from one dollar fifty for any job that I do here, my son! So, you owe me fifty cents already if I keep this one."

You turn on your heel and walk away - dejectedly. When you turn around you see the cobbler caressing his goatie and a wicked smile crossing his lips.

On line with Mom

Oscar Gwiriri

(Translated from Shona by Oscar Gwiriri)

I kept laying handholding the cellphone whilst resting it on my chest. I was dumbfounded and my mind seemed to have frozen. Can you imagine how mom was so hash on me? When she cut off the line, that's when I threw myself on the bed. I started recalling the tele-conversation and my heart ached as if it was in a frying pan.

"Son, since you are in the vicinity of your father, we rely on you on his checkup. You are quite aware that your father is always on-and-off health wise, but he had to travel anyway. We were initially worried, but got consoled after realizing that you are in Jo-burg where he was travelling to. Your father is old enough to retire, though he keeps on going to work. Anyway, he has to work for his family. It was his choice to have such a big family," Mother proclaimed. Her proclamation shocked me.

"It's ok Mom," I said.

"You must keep an eye on him and try to ascertain whatever is troubling him so that we all take charge in giving him solace. I believe you are quite aware that people of that age need love and being cared for. Therefore, I am giving you a task to find out what could be irritating him resulting in this continuous hypertension shoot out. If we don't take that move, we will lose the man. Once he is gone, we will be doomed, and this family would have lost the father figure. You know how your uncles treat us. Just imagine, once your father touches ground here, they all flock into our house expecting gifts and presents. We rarely have our own time all because of their presence. I really wonder. Therefore, my son, take care of your father. It's now every family member's duty to ensure that he is alright, otherwise the man will be no more."

"I get you clearly Mom. In reference to what you have said about identifying his worries, I have since noticed that there is something boggling his mind as we were relaxing yesterday night." I advised.

"That's it! You are quite on track on what I want us to do. What could be the problem affecting him, my dear?" Mother asked attentively. I could even feel her concern over the line.

"There is this issue about your plan to dispose ten cattle to raise funds for your holiday air ticket to Dubai. That issue is troubl…"

"What! Since when have you started interfering in parents' issues? What's wrong with you! How dare you get in between your father and me? You have gone out of bounds for sure. No wonder why I always caution you that once I'm dead, you will be in for it. My aggrieved spirit will haunt you for sure. Not even a single day have I ever got peace all because of you my children," Mother shouted. Her heavy sigh over the phone almost blasted my eardrum. There was silence for a while. I got worried that she could have collapsed out of anger.

"Mom! Mom! Mom! Mom are you there?"

"So you think I'm dead?"

"I'm sorry Mom! It's never been my intention to interfere in your affairs, but…"

"But what! I believe your damn stupid father could have influenced you. Isn't it?" She asked. I was lost of remorseful words. I knew my mother's behaviour quite well, once irritated; she could go berserk like a wounded buffalo.

"Not really Mom!" I answered.

"So what's all the fuss about?"

"I just considered that since you want us to know what's troubl…"

"What?"

27

"I'm so sorry Mom, but as you had advised that I must find out what's bothering father, then I just thought it's one of them. Father was suggesting that if you could hold on for a while so that the cattle multiply, than disposing the ten out of the dozen which…"

"You people don't irritate me, okay! I am not going to listen to any of you at all. As far as I am concerned, that Dubai trip is an obvious and unstoppable whirlwind. If that is what is affecting him, he can go hang. Nonsense! I wish you people could stay out of my way," She sighed heavily. I was shock-stricken by her position. My heart was broken to an extent whereby I felt as if the top floors of the flat I lodged had crumpled on me. I failed to get an appropriate response

She continued, "What's all your worry about disposing the cattle when they multiplied from the first two? Those two which will be left will still multiple anyway. I am disappointed by how you take your father's side. I am supposed to be taken care of and spoilt by my children like other parents are experiencing, but none of you ever does so, yet it is my right as a parent. Some parents are flying all over the world on trips sponsored by their lovely children and some of their children even compete to show their love, but as for me, I don't get even a sweet. Why do my own kids treat me like a barren woman? Most congregants put on new clothes throughout for half a year, but as for me, it's the same clothes every church day. Some of them are driving luxurious and expensive cars, and they splash mud on me as they drive past whilst I'm walking to and from church. All of you my children, you mean you can't even afford a wheelbarrow which may be handy to carry me to the main road to board a lift to hospital when I fall very sick? All parents need the attention of their children, who doesn't want it? Anyway, whom can I share this grievance, orphaned as I am? I bet, once I die, all of you will be in for it because of the way you are neglecting me. As for you, I have suffered a lot for your sake. I sent you to boarding school and spent my paltry funds in the view that you would take care of me, but it was a mere waste of money. Had I spent that on my air tickets the better. I sent you to university to study, and you brought about that silly wife of yours who was sick-and-tired of mischief. Instead of studying and fulfilling the purpose of going to university, that men-monger fooled you into a marriage of convenience. Therefore, as I make my plans, I don't want anybody to stand in my way. Do you understand me! I don't like what you have done, and it must cease forthwith from today onwards." Mom complained. She cut off the line.

"Mom! Mom! Mom are you there?" I flip flopped my cellphone to check if the network was still connected. I tried to call once again, but her phone was switched off.

DREAMS OLD WOMEN HAVE

Yeukai 'Mimyie' Benhura

When I walked into room 99, I was greeted by a putrid stench that dizzied me for a moment. I could hear her simultaneously chewing loudly and farting. The curtains were drawn and the room was as dark as night. I could barely see her as she lay on the bed. I walked straight towards the windows and pulled open the curtains and windows in a fury.

She squealed in agony as the light blinded her and I had to suppress a smile. I had just won my first victory. I turned back and studied her for a moment. She was lying on the ruffled bed, partly covered by the blankets, and her small frame was almost swallowed by the bed. She wore a pale peach bathrobe and a colourful headscarf. Her head rested on one arm and the other was placed on her hip. The arm looked bony and dry but there was a queer elegance to her pose.

She paid no heed to me, and slowly kept chewing some tree bark. Saliva mixed with the bark drooled from the corners of her mouth and she did not bother to wipe it off. When she finished chewing, she spat the remains on the floor. It was brown with a hint of green. She wiped her mouth with an upturned hand, cleaned off the residue and tidied her hand on her pink bed cover. If I had been less determined I would have quit in that moment.

"My name is Anita. What is yours?" I knew what her name was, but I had to gain control from the beginning. She looked up at me and scoffed, it was a long ten seconds before she answered.

"Suga!" she spat out as if it were rancid on her tongue.

"Now, Suga, I will be your aide for this month and, unlike the others, I will not tolerate any misbehaviour from you. Do we understand each other?"

She shrugged again, rose to sit up in her bed and began fluffing it, ignoring me.

"While I appreciate the implied meaning of your little act just now, I expect you to verbalise all communication. You are not a child so do not act as one. Understood?"

She gave me a cold stare, gritted what was left of her teeth and growled a 'yes' in response.

"Excellent." I began to tidy up her room, by picking up clothes strewn all over the floor, folding them neatly and packing them back into her closet.

"I have heard about you," I said, as I brought order to the room. I spoke about what I had heard about her and on occasion witnessed. I wanted her to know that I was not intimidated by her, but honestly I was. "You have terrorised everyone you have encountered in this institution since you arrived. There is no other resident as hated as you. The director was forced to make you a shared burden after you had harassed all your assigned aides. No one wants to take care of you, Suga, because somehow you feel it is okay to misbehave, insult and harass us. We even voted to have you chased out of the centre."

She clucked, almost as if she would be happy to be chased out of the centre.

Mama Suga,
She is a troubled soul,
A fiend walking among the living.
Tormenting all who cross her path,
Showing no remorse for her deeds.

"I will not let you torment me," I continued, "because I need this job. Mama Suga, you are not the only one haunted by the losses of the past. My father abandoned my mother when I was six, and she raised us alone. My brother, Amos Hanga, the big singer, I am sure you have heard his songs on the radio, left us when I was eighteen and never looked back. In the same year my brother Amos left, Mama had an accident that left her crippled. I need this job, Suga. I am all my family has."

I had no idea why I was telling her all my problems, but she needed to know what her actions would reap.

She began cleaning her fingernails, as if I was not in the room.

Not wanting to seem vulnerable,
She becomes a minx.
Her naughtiness is worse than that of a child,
She plays pranks on her aides,
Hurls profanities at anyone close enough to hear.

'Do you remember Siki? The aide you had last month. You traumatised her so much that she quit her job. If I remember correctly she said, you told her, 'Bring your man to me and I will show him what a real woman looks like.' Do you have any idea how much you hurt that poor woman?" I looked at her, waiting for her response, but she shrugged and began biting her nails and spitting them in my direction. My palm itched and I stopped myself from reaching out to slap her.

"Suga, that poor woman was having problems with her husband, which I am sure you and the rest of the centre know about. In less than a week after her husband's mistress came here and caused a scene, you decided to humiliate her like that? Did life not teach you to protect your sisters? You are a cruel woman, Suga." I hoped for some remorse but she giggled. She clearly was not bothered by what I was saying, but I would continue. I was bound to hit a nerve soon enough.

Our silence was broken by a loud rap on the door that drew my attention away from her. The knock was followed by Tendai's popping her head in, but she quickly retreated. I had no option but to follow her outside to hear what she wanted.

Be wary as you change her bed pan,
She will crank herself up and release a fart that will stink up the whole ward.
We should stop feeding her those boiled eggs!
Sometimes she is a true bad hat,
Purposely humiliating any who dare come close,
And pour her bed pan urine on them.

I did not bother to excuse myself from mama Suga, I just dashed out of the room. I found Tendai standing with arms akimbo and frowning next to Natsai, who was busy texting. I figured why they had come.

"If you guys are here to warn me about mama Suga," I said, "I already know about her well enough. There is no need for you to worry about me, I will survive my time with her. It is just a month after all."

"Why did you not ask Thomas to excuse you from taking up the duty? He has the authority to go against the stupid coin toss. You know what she did to me, how can you go ahead with it?" Tendai's voice was high pitched and squeaky when she was agitated. Natsai had raised her head from her phone and was laughing, only because she had not yet faced Mama Suga.

"Who can forget what happened to you, Tendai? If you had not let her see that you were afraid she would have never done anything. So far you are the only one on whom she has poured urine. Thank God for Thomas, you would have never survived day two with her, that I am sure of." Natsai was laughing loudly that the other residents began complaining in their rooms.

"Natsai, quiet! Tendai, I am glad that Thomas assisted you when you were put through the wringer, but I refuse to use my boyfriend's authority to make my life easier." With that, Tendai just shrugged and walked away.

"You know how she was treated by the old witch that is why she is so aggressive. You are the sweetest of us three that is why she is so overprotective of you. Talk to Thomas he will get you out of the duty. You are not strong enough to handle the drama. We are saying this because we care about you, just think about it dear." With that, Natsai also walked away, and left me wondering what I was trying to prove by going head to head with the most hated old woman at the centre.

"Was that the little mouse who liked to bath in my urine?" She asked as I walked in. I gave her a cold stare which only enticed her to attack even more.

"She even smiled when she had a taste of it, licked her lips even. That one was a good sport. She cried easily and lost her temper often. I like them irritable and wild and she was just perfect. If it was not for Mr Thomas who came to talk to me after she threatened to quit, I would have had more fun." She sounded pleased with herself.

"Will you shut up!" I screamed before I could stop myself.

"Oh, so you are like her."

I had two options, either to continue with my tantrum or to speak in a calmer tone but either way I was under her control and she was winning. I decided not to argue and carried on with folding her clothes.

She also fell silent.

Moments later she hoisted herself up from the bed groaning from the pains that ailed her, and I was almost tempted to run and assist her but I refrained from doing so. I was not going to show the fiend mercy. She dragged her feet across to the window, sat on her chair and stared outside with her back to me.

"So they are letting you marry that white boy of yours?" She asked when she was settled in her chair. Her voice was almost a whisper, like she was expressing an inner thought.

On the good days you see her staring out the window,
Dreaming of a life she lost,
But accepting comfort in having survived the losses.
Only her lips hint at rare moments of joy

It took me a moment to digest her question, yet I still did not realise her meaning. I looked at her reflection in the mirror, she looked in agony and strain like she had something weighing down on her soul. I was tempted to feel sorry for her, to actually directly blame myself for her meanness for whatever happened in her past.

'What did you say, Suga?" I asked her with a slight, and unintentional softness in my voice, which I regretted immediately.

"I asked why they will let you marry that white boy, Thomas, when they would not let me marry my Johnny."

The question shocked me because I had never thought of him as a white man. Just as a man. Then I quickly also realised Suga's meaning. She had taken an active role in the Second Chimurenga, the liberation struggle against the colonisers and during her time, interracial marriages were taboo. I wondered how she had failed to see that things had changed since independence. I was also curious to know who this Johnny was, but I was sure if I asked she would shut down.

I walked over to her bed and began to put fresh linen on it without responding to her question. She did not say anything but instead moaned and from the corner of my eye I saw her wipe tears off quickly. Or maybe she needed a little encouragement. I still had my reservations about being kind to her after she had harassed everyone else.

"Mama Suga, what happened with your Johnny?" I spoke softly.

She sat in silence tears streaming down her parched cheeks. She let them flow freely without a single sob. I let her mourn her past, she had clearly lost so much and had held in the pain for too long.

The voices from the past haunt her,
Her fist clenches and you know the wailing has begun.
She mourns for her life past,
A life filled with regret and shame.

"They came and took us from home when I was fifteen. Already at that time I had left school because no one wanted an educated wife and also the times were hard for my family. When they came I was excited to be a part of the heroes that sacrificed their lives for our country, I never knew in what way I was expected to sacrifice my life." She cleared her throat and I rushed to get her some water.

"We were taken to the base, and taught how to use guns, grenades and knives for close combat. This training lasted a few weeks, then one night Comrade Singer came and woke a few of us, loaded us into a truck and we were taken to the capital city, Salisbury. It was a long, silent drive, because we realised what part in the war we were about to play." She stopped and looked out the window.

She gently caressed her face as if she were reading a message imprinted on the wrinkles on her face. She placed her left fingers on her lips and began sobbing softly. The woman had a lot of hurt hidden within, and my relationship with Thomas must have caused some release. It was hard to hate her now. I was filled with curiosity and sympathy for her.

She yearns the memories lost,
Her eyes squinted in search for a better view.
She yearns for the beautiful views ages gone.
Her lips pursed longing long for the kiss only life gave,
What those lips have tasted, only they can testify!

"The comrades had selected the few beautiful ones of us to act as spies. It was well known that some of the white soldiers had acquired a liking for the black girls, so we were used to gain information from these soldiers. We went through training on how to be prostitutes, cleaners, laundry maids and baby sitters in targeted areas. I was placed as a cleaner in Major Luke Robertson's house. My job was to clean while I eavesdropped on all conversations that were made concerning the war." All this while she had spoken with her back to me. Now, she stood up and reached out her hand to ask for assistance.

I noticed a tiny gold ring that had what looked like an emerald stone on her ring finger. Spending time with Thomas I had become acquainted with fine jewellery. I wondered if this Johnny had given it to her.

"You wonder if it's the real thing," she chuckled. "It is very real. My Johnny gave it to me when he proposed. I had been in Major Robertson's employment for about six months when his handsome son Johnny arrived from England where he had been attending university. I will never forget the day I met him because that is the day I began to live." She giggled like a teenager in love, I knew how she must have felt because I felt the same way about Thomas.

Her back arched,
With old age and toils of her youth.
Her hands roughened,
Tremble as she reaches to feel the wrinkles on her once beautiful face.
She must have caused quite the stir in her day.

"I was treated like a slave by the Major and his household, and this hardly changed with the arrival of Johnny. He was the only one who showed me any sympathy. He often saw his mother abuse me and he would come to comfort me in private. We were innocent and chaste in our love that remained undeclared for the longest while. On my days off, I would go and report any news I had and afterwards I would meet him at a cottage owned by one of his friends' family. They were more sympathetic to the black man's plight." She smiled so sweetly. I knew the memories were wonderful.

"You have never known a love more beautiful than forbidden love. We flourished in our love, sneaking behind his family and my superiors. We were on opposite sides of the war and we had no right to be so. On the day he proposed, I had been beaten with a wooden spoon on my back at his mother's orders. The whole household heard my screams and he had saved me. In that moment, I knew he loved me. He fought with his parents about the insubordination and suddenly proposed to me before his parents and the staff. Of course I said yes, even though I knew we were both being silly. The other staff all clapped their hands in excitement and his mother slapped me straight across the face. I had expected some form of resistance but not a slap. From that moment, it all became chaotic." I felt her heartbreak.

Some days she has nightmares.

She wakes up screaming and drenched in sweat,
Lost in her previous life.

"That moment is the source of all the nightmares I get at night. I knew they did not like me because of my skin colour, my position in society, but I never knew anyone could be capable of such hatred for another human being. I never chose to be as I was and neither did Johnny, we were merely victims of God's creation, that he made in his own image. How cruelly dissimilar his image is."

She mutters under her breath,
When she does not get her way
Mischief and pain are an artwork that nature painted on her face

"His mother dragged me out of the house by my apron and skirts. She shouted vulgarities at me, his father stood there and watched. Jonny screamed at his mother to stop and his father punched him in the face. She demanded the ring, I refused to part with it, ran from the house, and headed to the base. There, I found the commander waiting for me and he paraded me as a traitor. The comrades took turns kicking and punching me until I passed out. When I woke up, I was lying in a forest in Mount Selinda with broken ribs and swollen eyes. From that moment I knew I had to hide from the comrades all my life because if they found out I was still alive, they would kill me."

"Is that why you fought so hard not to be taken in by the guards the day they found you?"

"Yes, it has become so hard for me to trust even the people of my own kind. I fear for my life and I have no idea why I just shared my story with you." She looked so vulnerable that I could see all the pain she had been carrying all her life melt away.

39

"Do you know what happened to your Johnny, Mama? Did you ever find him?"

"No. I never dared to go back and look for him. He was lost to me from that day. I still love him even after all these years. I got a job as a house maid at a farm just outside Harare, owned by a white couple. With the new government, their farm was taken and they left for England. I was left homeless and jobless. I then moved to Harare and moved from one maid job to another until I was too old to be employed. I never saw my family and never married because I was waiting for my Johnny."

"Maybe we can look for him, Mama. Would you like that?" She nodded in response and I went to sit by her as we spoke of her Johnny and my plans to find him.

THE BLACK CAT

Phumulani Chipandambira

We sadly woke up, our feet nibbled. Simba was very angry and he suggested that we must kill the black fat cat.

Rats had feasted on us that previous night. Rats do not easily fall into traps.

"He is too lazy," Simba shouted "Hitler deserves death!"

Papa named it Hitler because of its whiskers and brown eyes. Hitler was one of its kind. I hate cats but Papa likes them. He loves pets, he always let Shumba, the dog, eat the left-overs from his china plate. Mama complained about it but Papa never listened.

We looked for it in all places, we searched in the bedroom, inside the shack that we use as the kitchen, in the pit latrine, we searched everywhere, but we could not locate it.

It was still early for it to wander into the neighbourhood, the sun had risen, its rays licking the Katanga township, making our shadows appear too long. Mama had risen early and went out, when we were still asleep.

We knew she would not come back till noon. She is a hawker, she sells floor polish and brooms every morning. Papa did not sleep at home once again, he was out on one of his numerous beer drinking errands.

It took us two hours to find it. We found it sleeping under the shade of the green banana tree leaves, relaxed. Hitler had a shinning black fur, it walked with feline grace. It also refused to eat dirty and raw things. It was very different from the mangy cats that stay at the dumpsite.

"Let us starve it before we hang it," I suggested.

"Oh no lets sell it," Simba shouted.

41

"Nobody buys a black cat. What if we dump it at the shops," I suggested.

Simba knew that l was afraid of killing it. He teased me many times, saying that I cannot even kill a cockroach and he called me a coward of the cowards.

Dumping a cat was not also easier. We had to put it in a sack, tie it at the top and walk without turning back. We would then leave the sack in the forest or at the crossroads.

"Oh, no! Let's kill it!" Simba brushed my idea aside.

Hitler looked at us with its big brown eyes as big as Mama's raincoat buttons. Simba patted it softly on its back, grabbed it on the neck and quickly shoved it under the upturned metal dish. l wondered what was he up to. He sat on top of the dish and the cat mewed and scratched the insides of the dish.

"Do you want to suffocate it?" l asked and he said "No, come and sit here."

My mind was puzzled and I thought he wanted to kill it by knifing it at the throat like what Mama always do when slaughtering the chickens.

He fetched a stone and two big sticks and I waited pondering what if he was possessed and being tormented by the unrelenting demons. He drummed the dish once and the cat that had relaxed began to scratch the insides of a metal dish, it was a futile attempt to free itself for the dish was too big. It was a big dish that l could not lift on my own.

"Lets sing and dance " Simba shouted. "Sing Nyasha ! Sing, I shot the Sherif" he cried. Bob Marley is Papa's best musician, he once said his music heals the poor man's soul.

"Simba please, lets leave it alone" I was no longer interested in his games.

"Come on Nyasha, be a man," he drummed to the tune of reggae and what I could do was to jump up and down. I could not shake my waist. Papa sometimes danced like that, he had started to keep long hair. Neighbours teased us by calling to us "Rasta-children".

He drummed the upturned dish for so long. I stopped dancing when I felt tired. "Simba that's enough", I shouted. Simba stubbornly remained sitted and continued on drumming the metal dish. He then stood up from the metal dish and followed me onto the streets to play with other boys.

We played the ball of rags and we forgot about Hitler, our black cat that wore a purple ribbon around its neck.

We later learnt that it was a taboo to kill a black cat- *felicide*. A cat dies thousands time before its actual death.

When we returned to our house, I lifted the dish and the cat fled blindly. It hit the fence, picked itself and ran along the street before it disappeared around the bend.

Simba fell down with laughter.

Since that day we never saw it again. It never returned. Those who saw it running said that it looked like a black veldt hare.

When Mama came back home from her routines, she was very tired of walking. "Did you two feed Hitler and Shumba with yesterday's left-overs?" she asked.

"Yes, Mama" Simba lied!

We took the plates and dishes to the sink and we began to eat the left-overs. *Makoko!*

The unknown b

Mushumbi Aaron F

He thinks, they will be never enough time to read. This thought asphyxiate him. Aaron. A gentleman in his late thirties. He suffers from myopia and utopia. His world is only the books he reads through the night. Endlessly and everyday and he is insatiable. An avid reader. He has lost contact with reality. The books are his reality and the reality his books. A hopeless situation. He shivers – craving – for books. Premature greying hair on his head. Short, not well-groomed hair. He does not drink strong beverages. Neither does he smoke crack. Nor knowledge of the birth canal. Aaron thinks himself levitical. Perpetual vows on poverty – will explain – vows on chastity, also an explanandum.

To the right and left of his studying desk there are photogenic pictures of beautiful girls. Women. There is a difference in meaning between girls and women. Girls are full of sugar, but can't resist that women are also full of sugar. One picture, a dark, perfect giant. In navy jeans, tight on her and a dubious smile. Pensively staring at the camera lenses before the shatter goes off. Aaron has non to it. Its philosophy. Axiology. Too good a case study of mermaids and copulation. Appetising. His father a canonist and are friends and alike. His father's superstitions of witches that bewitched gran gran. His philial milipeding or dried caterpillar especially in freezing weather. She is expensive in outlook and Aaron dares not describe the inlook. Colours dangerously beautiful. Detoured colours and in descript. One can just say good. His mother high pitched in voice. Explanans.

Finding the missing number. Aaron is a primary school teacher – who learnt pedagogies in the dog days of political consciousness. Kind of congregants refusing to paean any more. Same age – but he was thrown in the gallows for a decade and came back detached from the world – nostalgia thinking 2019 is 1998 and can't move from there. A mental incurable disease and though weaned his mother takes care of him on that aspect or he will think he is still six. He doesn't know that. Two; four; b and eight. Six makes sense. For juveniles with a democratic teacher like Syllabus A prescribes as the best. And it's permissible. Bread and butter for the poor. Teachers, nurses, police.

Two; ten; twenty five; fifty escalating and sky rocketing. An egg. Homeward. Five hundred; five hundred and one. They like that topic. Numbers. And one of the objectives is to say, write and read numbers in words and digits. And Aaron gives them endless notes. Descriptive and not defunct. The kind of thinking in its simplest, original and best form is the brain child of Margret Artwood – *The Blind Assassin*. And Aaron was reading, *Agent in Place* by Helen – she is good again, but gained that he will not venture into politics or spy business or any form of intelligence and diplomacy. Dirty. He loves his life. Very. Shelves and shelves of books. Thick copies. And Mandela dug his own grave in *No Easy Walk to Freedom*. Aaron is departing for Harare on Saturday, seething for Daniele Steele. These girls are the definition of seduction and Marechera fucked his female character in a story he was writing. Mad.

They understand. Pa was true. And Ma. Aaron discovered the definition of Kleptomania and it placed him right on track US$ 50 on 100 rtgs its everything and she was smiling ruby red lips. Dark pupilled eyes. A doll. Aaron playing chess and castling and piercing bewildered shouts – from nowhere and shivering and an erection, bad combination and eureka. Plays no more, where the hell *Black Sunlight* at 100 pounds. The smile was good, but she refused to kiss him. Is that what you want, it will be censored. There and then.

He likes his mother because her marginal propensity to consume is very low and good. And her marginal propensity to save is good. Basics. That is mealie gruel. He has a strong appetite for meat. And leadership is intelligent. He is reading philosophy and will go to law. *The Communist Manifesto*, introduction to politics. He does not know

– what they say about cold blooded murderer – but he read briefly culpable homicide and soft skull theory. Philosophy, that is of science say theology is meaningless and poetry and literature and he agrees. I want to give people bread and flowers. Let me sleep. The theory of Thomas Kahn or maybe falseability – if the road leads to Mbare, home of Povo, then you are a hero. He doesn't have any original opinion on that as is the explanation I have promised.

The girl or the woman as we have agreed says, his opinions are not fine and researched. Complete strangers, but next of skin when the weather is fine. Too bookish. But detested anarchism, maybe intellectual. The other picture well photoshopped depicting a pleasant girl in white not very tights. He asked her if she played him, but could not get to the bottom of the story. She didn't smile. Massive another definition of the unknown b.

20/06/2019   2035 mutukwana no electricity

Seven
Matthew K Chikono

Last Friday evening I came back from work and found Flora cooking supper. A tantalising smell of beef stew struck my nose as I entered the kitchen and there she was, in her pink satin dress looking a decade younger and more beautiful than ever. Stirring the Sadza in the favorite black pot, she smiled and told me that dinner would be ready in a few minutes. Before she could order me out of the kitchen, I went out to clean up before dinner was served. When I came back, I found her in front of the black oven, taking out those hot lemon scones I like very much. I won't lie, it was the best meal I have ever had in a very long time. Flora had been dead for seven months.

"Seven years," Chamunorwa always whispers in my ear, "Flora has been dead for seven years Gilbert."

He is my friend and he loves me. I am sure he does, I mean how can he be my best friend for seventy years and not get crazy. It must be seventy years including those years our mothers were pregnant teenagers. My earliest memory of us is that of us both dressed in napkins made of old torn shirts, pooping together in my mother's kitchen. We might have been two or three years old. Alas, there were no cameras, to preserve these rare memories.

He is old, so am I, but he looks the youngest among the trio of us. An old greyish wool hat sits on his head, donning a peculiar smile on his naked gums and a huge waistcoat I gave him on his third wedding seventeen years ago. Chamunorwa always gulps down some millet beer he thinks or says anything worth your time. He believes that the masese is the real and only poison that had kept him alive all these years. I like him, I have to like him or else I will be friendless for the remainder of my days which unfortunately are not much now.

"Seven years," Chamunorwa whispers in my ear, "Flora has been dead for seven years Gilbert."

We are sitting outside Zvidozvevanhu beerhall on a Sunday evening. At least it's a cool day, I am always cold these days and I hate it. The people of Chitungwiza are rushing to the vegetable stalls to buy the fresh ingredients of their supper in the process raising unnecessary dust. It hasn't rained in a while and we are choking with the dust but what else can we do, we are old men with nothing else to do.

"Seven years," Chamunorwa whispers in my again in my left ear, "Flora has been late for seven years my dearest friend."

There is no need to whisper the beerhall is empty, it's always empty. Young people don't drink here, they never will. They prefer night clubs or the new fancy sports bar next door were modern music is played too loud.

They don't play loud music in Zvidozvevanhu beerhall nor do they play music at all. This beerhall is old, we have been drinking here since we were teenagers. I like it nothing ever changes in here. It's always empty and quiet and I always tell Chamunorwa not to whisper but he always does, old habits never die at all.

"Yes, seven years," I mutter with embarrassment, "My wife has been dead for seven years."

I cannot bear to think what they are thinking of me; a man who doesn't remember how long his wife has been late. I might not remember how long it was but I know all the pain I went through. She didn't die peacefully in her bed while I sat beside her holding her hand, no. She was electrocuted to death.

The old power lines ran underneath our backyard and one stormy afternoon, Flora walked barefooted on top of an exposed wire. I was watching her walk away from me, I hated it but she always made it beautiful. She never screamed. Her body was thrown few metres away. I saw smoke coming out from every part of her before the smell of burning flesh hit my nose. I raced to save my wife. I ran to my beloved Flora and there was nothing else to be done except cover her body and weep. She was 62.

"Yes, seven years," I mutter with embarrassment, "My wife has been dead for seven years."

Not that I am proud but I have to say I am the smartest and the most intelligent of my friends and it is unheard of me to forget anything. I cannot even blame alcohol, I have never taken it in my life. It is definitely strange that I would forget that it has been seven years since I saw Flora die. In Zimbabwe load shedding is up to 18 hours a day and on average less than five people die because of electrical shocks. To the world Flora is now just part of statistics, a mere number that saves no purpose to those who loved her. It is a terrible way to die and a horrible way to lose your soulmate.

"Yes, seven years sure," I mutter with shame and embarrassment, "My wife has been late for seven years and it's unbelievable that I forgot the day my wife of fifty years passed away."

We meet at Nyadire teacher's college where we were both students in the late 50s.

"My name is Flora, just like Roman goddess of flowers." That was the first thing she said as she sat down next to me in the school library and I was in love. I have told this story a million times before that I am starting to believe it's true. It's not. Everyone thinks it's the best love story ever told, even Flora thought it sweet for the rest of her life. I can't say I lied, I only simplified the story.

She was in her first year and I was in my third and final year of our teaching diplomas when I first noticed her in the library. She was a bookworm and I was just an avid reader who wanted to read half of the books in the library. She always sat on the chair next to Shona fiction section. Honestly all the books I had read weren't of any help on how I could talk to her. I did the only other thing that I thought was romantic, I sat on her chair one day.

"You are sitting on my chair."

"I am sorry?" I pretended to be surprised, "This chair and everything that is within this library belongs to the school, are you aware of that?"

I could see it in her eyes that she knew but she didn't care, all she wanted was the perfect reading spot.

"You are Flora, right?" I asked with a false dawn of recognition on my face, "Flora like the Roman goddess of flowers."

She wore a white blouse and a toe length coloured skirt that day. Sockless she wore a semi-heeled black shoe. Her hair was cut short and huge specs covered her eyes. She was just an angel that had recently lost its wings.

"I sit here every day reading and you can pack your things and leave, it will make things easier for everyone."

"Yes Chloris!" I continued with our deep philosophical chat, "Chloris is her Greek counterpart, by the way will you marry me?"

"Yes!" she gladly answered six years later after I had asked for the dozenth time. We got married and lived happily ever after.

"So, you are saying your wife came back from the dead and is now cooking delicious food for you?" Chamunorwa asks as an afterthought, his attention more focused on the beer than the question.

"No, he said his dead wife is alive," says our other companion whom I think is crazy, "I think he is crazy."

Tichafara is not our friend but he is always there for us for a very long time. We got acquainted when he first decided to spend his Sundays drinking beer at our bar than spend it at a local baptist church where he was a pastor.

"My wife came back to me," I calmly say, "she is well and alive."

"Mwariwe!" Chamunorwa chokes in disbelief, "Don't tell me you visited Sekuru Ngara?"

"Sekuru Ngara the witch?"

"No, Sekuru Ngara the healer."

"Same thing." Tichafara says spitting, "that old man is no good."

He spits again. Tichafara hates Sekuru Ngara that's not a secret. A physical fight between the two had resulted in Tichafara losing his job as a pastor. No one knows what the argument was all about.

"Tell me Gilbert," Chamunorwa says removing his hat, "what did that man give you?"

"Or worse, what did he do to you?"

"Nothing," I say to them with my magic smile, "he just told me to go home."

From the way they are looking at me I can tell they don't believe me, they will never do.

"Fine," I sigh, "he told me to bath in the Nyatsime River at midnight for seven nights."

"In this kind of weather?"

"Bathing in the cold river was the act necessary to test your dedication and commitment. It was an act of faith and you passed. Now tell us, what did you pay for it?" Tichafara says thoughtfully. He is clever and I really thank God that Tichafara doesn't believe in God anymore, how else would I learn this deep philosophical stuff from this man? I honestly believe that his efforts would have been wasted on those church people if he had continued preaching at the church, modern Christians deserve to go to hell after all.

"Tichafara, Gilbert has just been given some witchcraft or worse, a spiritual wife and we need to help him!"

"Or maybe the little headache hasn't gone away yet dear Chamunorwa."

Oh yes, my little headache. My friends call it a little headache but it's worse, psychosis. I have been diagnosed of it for a while but I am fine, I think I am fine. Flora is back, do I have to care if it's the psychosis or the medicine Sekuru Ngara gave me? No, I am happy. I have everything I desire although it's just for seven days. My friends bewail around me and I sip my mahewu silently, patiently waiting for Flora to come back to me for another seven nights.

STRANGE THINGS HAPPEN

Christopher Kudyahakudadirwe

A wintry wind whistles through the weary willow trees behind us. The cold seems to have been dragging on for far too long than usual this season. A few clouds sail across the blue sky like white water-lily leaves on the surface of a blue pool. Although the temperatures are low, the day is bright with the sun being blocked in short episodes by the north-westerly bound clouds. The air smells sterile except for the slight whiff of perfume that drifts from the lady who stands next to me.

For as long as we have been standing here, the lady has not turned to look at me but that does not stop me from looking at her through the corner of my eye. It is not my making that I should be standing here, but my friend and his wife called me to come and be with them as they address the young people gathered here with whom they were to go on an excursion. I am to make my mind as to join them later. A good number of the youths have gathered and are standing in groups of twos and threes on the open ground before us, chatting to one another animatedly about the trip – so I think – as I am not close enough to hear the subject of their bubbling. We are waiting for all the boys and girls to arrive.

"Max," I turn to my friend who is standing between the lady and his wife on the other side.

"What time do you expect everyone to be here?"

"We told them to be here by 10am." He looks at his wrist. "And we still have half an hour before 10."

"Judging by the number already here, it would seem they will all arrive very soon." As if by infection, I also check my watch.

"Yes, and they are also very eager to climb the mountain." Max's wife chimes in.

The lady, whose name I later learnt to be Letwin, seems unbothered by neither the prevailing weather conditions nor the subject of our discourse at this moment. Like a horse with blinkers she kept her round face looking ahead, and I felt the invisible Berlin wall that she seems to maintain between us thickening. Since when have I been shy to look at the faces of ladies? This question keeps popping into my mind every time I take sneaked looks at her. These snuck glances at the young woman reward me with a rich garden of womanhood which has been endowed and nurtured on this human being.

"Max," I am almost sweating under the pressure of wanting to be alone with this lady and telling her about the riot of emotions raging in my mind. "I'll take Letwin to buy coffees at the service station over there. We'll be back soon, soon." I announce that as if I have already agreed with Letwin about going to the shop.

"That's okay. And please bring me a packet of cigarettes." He gives me some money.

Letwin did not disagree with my proposal for a walk away from Max and his wife, so we saunter from the couple like a couple that has been together for some time. She displays a dignified gaiety that is not common among women of her type. Now I can look at her face whose features are as sharp as if they were chiseled out of granite, with dark languid eyes filling their meant positions on her small round face. Small pimples grace her fair skin without much consequence. Her breasts are small lemons punctuating her steps with bounces that would entice anyone seeing them to want to harvest them and make lemonade. Like a winding staircase, I turn to check what is at her back; her rounded bum pronounce her an epitome of God's exquisite creation to its best – they bounce with each step in a way that make me want to forget that I am going forward.

So, with all this having been uploaded into my brain, we walk side by side for a while before none of us has garnered enough courage to speak. As it was my first time to see her, this could be the reason why I have found it difficult to summon much courage to speak to her. She has been presented to me without warning, and I am sure she also has the same foreboding feeling about speaking to me. So far, I have not heard her voice, but my ears are itching to pick the timbre of it.

"Let's get ourselves some coffees from the service station." I break the suffocating silence ultimately, forgetting that I had already announced this before we left where we had been standing with Max and his wife.

"I prefer cappuccino."

I raise my eyebrows. "You have a lovely voice."

She speaks like a cello played in an empty hall; all husky and deep-throated.

"Thank you. Not many people have said that to me." Letwin steals a glance at me for the first time. Her dark eyes sweep over my face like an unintended caress – a soft feather moved by the wind over my skin - as they quickly scan my features. How I wish I had the privilege to peer into their depths to fathom what dwells in them.

As we approach the service station, Letwin excuses herself to go and use the bathroom. I wait for her near the pumps. When she comes back, she has taken off the dress she was wearing and is now wearing a pinkish one. I do not know where she has put the previous one nor where the pinkish one had materialised from; perhaps she was wearing both dresses at one time. I do not say anything about that, but I look askance as to how that had happened, for she did not have a handbag that could fit any garment bigger than a handkerchief.

At the service station, we buy our drinks and the cigarettes for Max.

"May I have your cellular number?" I ask her knowing that when we get back to Max and his wife, I may forget to ask for it. Without hesitation, she takes out a pen from her purse and writes: 071 546 9199 on a page she tears from what looks like a diary. I take the paper

54

and put it in my pocket after looking at for a while. She smiles at me as she replaces her diary-like book into her purse and closes it.

As we walk back to Max, I imagine myself fondling her lemon-sized breasts and as stated before, making lemonade from them, and finally kissing her all over everywhere, but this cannot be done as I imagine because I am carrying the drinks in my hands and secondly, we have barely come to that level of knowing each other as to be allowed such luxuries. When we are about to get to where we left the others, I put down my coffee and go for what I am imagining. Letwin does not resist. Then I see Max coming around the corner and ... I wake up. I realised I am only dreaming!

*

I check the time on the wall clock. It is 06:29. I am late for work. I should have been up at 6 o'clock already. Quickly I get into the cold shower as if to extinguish all the fires that have been lit in the dream, throw clothes on and dash to the car to add to the traffic in the morning rush hour. I arrive at work at 08:17. After settling in my office, my mind runs over the details of the dream that I had. It is still so vivid. The face of Letwin is still imprinted in my mind, her softness still lingers in my fingers and her perfume is still wafting into my nose. The dream was so real. One thing that struck me is that the number she had written on that paper in the dream is still stuck in my mind. I immediately enter it in my phone book.

Work is sluggish: filing tax returns for the company, sending out emails to prospective customers and in between, cups and cups of coffee.

At 10, out of curiosity, I decide to call the number that Letwin had given me in the dream.

"Hello." A female voice answers from the other end.

"Hello, Letwin." I am just trying out that name since it belonged to the girl in the dream.

"How did you get my number?"

"You gave it to me … in- in a dream. Are you Letwin?"

"Which dream? That's impossible. You're lying. Who are you?"

"Perhaps." I sit up in the chair. "But that is what happened. I had a dream in which a girl named Letwin gave me her number." I am feeling stupid about the whole thing now. "It was so vivid that I remember the number even now. And for curiosity's sake I decided to dial it."

"Who are you?"

"Kudzi."

"Strange things are happening, if I'm to go by what you're telling me." There is a brief silence on the end of the line. "You must have got my number from someone who knows me. Where are you?"

"I'm in Mutare and you?"

"Chinhoyi."

"I've never been in Chinhoyi. According to my knowledge you could be the first person from there that I'm beginning to know."

My communication with Letwin is still going on. She has sent me pictures of herself and, good God, how she resembles the lady in my dreams! We're going to meet very soon. I've made a strong obligation to go and visit Chinhoyi in order to meet Letwin, this time not in a dream.

NOAH'S ARK
Sheila Banda

After being verbally massacred, his dignity torn into shreds, Farai salvaged his remains with a lump in his throat. He groped for the chair as a blind man does without a backward glance. He had prepared himself to sit but had remained suspended, trying to absorb the shock of it all. His shirt could not hold the strain as it found its way out of the trousers. The pressure being too much, Farai heaved his bulk upon the hard, rickety piece of furniture which creaked for mercy. His misplaced shirt exposed charcoal black occupants epitomising two hot buns buckling under pressure. He felt much heavier as the weight of humiliation was an added load to his gigantic frame. His troubled and disturbed mind kept him fidgeting throughout the remaining minutes of the meeting. His sweat glands suddenly became more porous than before threatening to channel hot boiling blood moving in his veins. Anger, embarrassment, vengeance, bitterness mingled with fear was all bottled up in him.

The silence after this cutting edge episode was threatening. A pin drop could have produced an echo. Tension was so visible and tangible that one could tear off its fabric and produce a jacket out of it just to cover Farai's embarrassment. No one dared move. It was a bad moment frozen in time. Not a single whisper. People fumbled with their fingers, some were trying to remove their freshly painted nail polish. Some succeeded and the evidence was right on their skirts. Men were even straightening their trousers and trying to make them longer. Some were putting their askew ties back in place. Some were staring at their feet as if it was still a wonder to them how they could possess such beautiful things! Everyone was somewhere and busy but there feigning absentmindness. Only the howling wind you could hear. Trees swayed fiercely back and forth. Women's oily drenched wigs were violently torn from their heads exposing kinky

57

unkempt hair. Leaves were strewn all over the congregantes. Sand grains were thrown in people's faces but no one dared complain. Women took cover under their "zambias" whilst men shielded themselves with their hands, heads bowed down. Dark grey clouds were looming in the distance threatening to burst any time soon. Animals were scurrying about for cover sensing imminent danger. The weather, the tension, painted a gloomy picture.

All this while, Monica seemed to be perusing her notes. She did it slowly and carefully as if waiting for something to happen for her to stop this monotonous action. It was a diversion from her thoughts. It was a distraction. She had expected an outburst from the mighty, colossal Farai but instead got the shock of her life. Silence. The Surrender, the buckling in was something she did not envisage. Was this a conquest to be celebrated over? Had she tamed the revered and honoured one with her only weapon and ammunition, her words? But this, this episode, this occurrence was an enigma she had to solve. Her nerves were all jittery but she would not for the sake of her pride and a minute long victory ever show it. What have I done? But she knew that when the elephants fight, the grass bear the brunt. She was going to be in this for the long haul and this was just the welcoming remarks. For now, she was in possession of the last laugh and she wondered how many last laughs she was going to pocket.

"Ahem", Monica cleared her throat, "I will handover to Mr Chairman to finalise the proceedings of this meeting. Mr Chigariro over to you." The short stout man leapt into action and took his Chairman's position. He bellowed into the microphone and his booming voice caught people off guard and shook them into reality.

"This meeting is adjourned", he said, "and we will advise of another meeting pending the results of the findings from our discussions. Minutes will be availed on a date still to be announced. Thank you for your contributions, concerns and for the time you invested in attending. Thank you for the unity of purpose for 'united we stand and divided we fall'. The war for development and transparency still continues 'aluta continua'. May you go in peace and stay in peace. Thank you!"

Responding to this dismissal, nursing mothers raptured their breasts from their suckling babes who howled in demonstration. Some were ridding themselves of dust accumulated courtesy of the windy weather. Everyone was hastening, men already quickening their pace for a heavy downpour was eminent. It was a long walk back to the village and only those in possession of vehicles were lingering about.

Farai was robbed of a dignified exit. He was left with a tail between his legs. His elite group feigned not to notice. Mr Chigariro was the first to approach him exchanging pleasantries and sharing tit bits about family life. People were mingling and such occasions stretched to unnecessary ridiculous long hours. Some would be weighing each other's progress and success and boasting about their achievements. Those waiting for free rides from their privileged counterparts were standing in their own group. These were typical wannabes who yearned to be associated with success although it was a long way from them. They had to endure the biting weather whilst discussing noneties and pretended not to be moved by the previous events.

Far out in the road, a cloud of dust trailed behind people hurrying to their respective homes. They were conversing along the way. You could hear cackles of laughter and clapping of palms in joy.

The once sombre gathering came into life. One gossip mongers, Mai Runyararo, voice was aloof,

"Askana today's events heeeei, God is there", clicking her fingers for emphasis, "Farai being cut down to size like that. God is for everyone and God is not a stupid!" Awhile, her plump hands resting on her heaving, bulging chest, she saw Gods goodness and vengeance in people's embarrassments, which was her inbuilt mechanism, a sadist in the making. No one in her presence would utter a sentence to support her for one day it would haunt you. Instead you could hear women chorusing 'yes, yes it's true' in response. Men were basing about in their baritones

"Surely each dog has its day. Mmmm Monica saying that to Farai amidst all of us, she is stepping on something surely. Something is brewing or has already been brewed. This should be written in the genus book of records I tell you." Baba Chikwavairo marvelled.

"I saw it from the first that Farai was no match for Monica. I said it and people thought I was just a jealous hare in the book only moved by the turning of pages! Hehehehe! Today my prophecy has been fulfilled."

"Iwee Samson, this time around you were right. They say what goes around comes around."

Such conversations were doing the rounds and people couldn't wait to relay the proceedings to those at home, those perturbed by the unfriendly weather. It began to drizzle and an appetising scent of wet soil rose into the atmosphere. The tempo increased. The heavily saturated clouds unleashed their anger on mother earth in great torrents. There was no place to scurry for cover for people had covered a distance. Umbrellas were raised in a bid to shield themselves from the downpour. Thunder rumbled, lightning cracked and the wind whipped away umbrellas and plastics held by feeble fingers.

Trees swayed and bent back and forth as if they would snap. Rain plummeted bare haired heads with such vigour as if it was a punishment for an unknown offence. Ladies held hands in unison for fear of being carried away in the maddening weather. You could hear 'maiwees' and cursing from people. They were drenched and soaked to the bone and the heavy downpour reduced their momentum and they were wadding about like ducks in the muddy terrain. Mother nature was in a rage and if this was an omen of things to come, at least they had seen better days.

Sekuru Chogugudza trailed far behind the chattering, excited and drenched people, his bent figure supported by his roughly craven walking stick. One could fear that his hands would be ripped off by the rough edges of the stick. No meeting would pass without his attendance nomatter how far the distance. The energy he possessed didn't equal his old age thus prompting villagers to align him to wizardly's powers. Word was his walking stick was actually an ominous python which sapped strength from villagers as they slept. His neighbour, though lazy in nature, concocted stories of how he saw the python draining blood from his deceased wife whilst Sekuru was standing straight and his face looking youthful with teeth full in his mouth grinning and urging on his 'lover', the python. This, he says happened a night before his wife passed on. But everyone knew how Mharapara loved chasing skirts as he liked chasing stories and brought the disease upon himself.

Sekuru had been a teacher once with ZJC a qualification and was not accustomed to have stale news brought to him. He was an informed and alert old man who had surpassed his former colleagues' life expectancy because of his wise ways. His grandchildren adored him and his children worshipped him. He retained most of his old ways and refused to embrace some modern ways his children wanted to enforce in him. His notion was that modernisation had driven young people into an early grave. The food which encouraged obesity and diseases associated with it, televisions which he labelled the devil incarnate as they spread immorality etc etc. He said back then in his time, girls used to be real girls and men used to be real men but nowadays the whole lot was like a bunch of crumpled and creasy second hand clothes from Mupedzanhamo (second hand clothes mall)!

"Tsk, tsk", he would click his tongue, "what an obscene generation."

As he trudged along in the downpour embracing God's gift upon earth and taking in every drop, he was mumbling to himself. In all the excitement and drama, no one offered a word of prayer to end the meeting. He marvelled at how this generation labelled themselves Christians and mocked the traditional ways. Suddenly a car pulled over just near sekuru. As the driver rolled down his window he recognised his great grandson, Tumai.

"Old boy come on in." with a loving smile plastered on his face. Sekuru walked gracefully to the opened door and took his seat.

"Life has been kind to you sekuru but you not as young as you used to be or want to be. Why walk all the way to the meeting and endanger yourself in this bloody weather?"

Every drop of water he had soaked was now dripping on the seat and forming a pool on the floor. He sneezed here and there for the warmth of his environment and his dampness was two opposing factors. Sekuru took his time before responding as was his character.

"Farai was ridiculed by Monica, his girlfriend because she is now his boss's mistress. Eey this life! A life of lost causes."

With that sekuru sealed his lips and sneezed violently as his body jerked forward in unison to the roaring thunder and whip of lightning. The car shook vigorously and Tumai applied brakes. He looked at his sekuru and couldn't help wonder how these signs exhibiting his approval or discontentment over something followed him. It was true what they said that with age comes wisdom, applied to though with some only wrinkles come with age.

"So what should be done sekuru to restore dignity to this life then?" Tumai asked

"Mwana wemuzukuru wangu, zvakaoma. (My great grandson, its mind boggling) We need Noah's ark."

"What? Noah's ar.... Why Sekuru?" Tumai couldn't finish his sentence coz he was perplexed at this unexpected response.

"That's what we need Tumi, that's the only solution." With that Sekuru rested his case and Tumai started the car and they travelled in silence until they reached their destination.

A Special Place
Matthew K Chikono

Two years after the Chimurenga war ended my older sister, Tilda, came back home. It was almost seven years since she had sneaked away from the house during a November stormy night. My mother had started believing that, somehow, she had found a way to join the freedom fighters across the border in Mozambique, and by the grace of the lord, she had perished with thousands of other young people fighting for the liberation of Zimbabwe. It was a lie of course, she didn't want to believe what my father said was a disgrace to the family; Tilda, the daughter of a strict village pastor and his wife who was a primary school headmistress, had ran away to Salisbury to indulge in wantonness and debaucheries only offered by the city. Well it didn't matter much though; she had finally come back home. She didn't come alone though, a six-year-old boy was in her tow.

They couldn't accept a bastard in their home, my parents said.

In a way they were right, Takura, for that was his name, was not ours to keep but his father's family. My father could not fathom the idea of keeping his daughter's embarrassment for the world to sneer and laugh at, that would have been rubbing salt to a fresh wound. I couldn't imagine what would happen to the pastor's famous fornication preaching in the village, if the pastor's own daughter could not follow them then who would? Before she had even unpacked her bags, the pastor was ready to kick her outside of his house. Tilda sobbed.

In their scaling of their daughter's morality they almost left out the most important thing; Takura was their grandson and my nephew too. His father might have been one of the countless men my sister associated with at the shebeen she worked at in the city or maybe one of the boys who had ran away to die in the war, my sister wasn't sure.

She was a whore who would burn in hell, my mother did not mince her words. Tilda wept.

Shedding tears for the plight of her child was something that made me believe Tilda genuinely loved her son and it struck my eyes and my mother's heart. The headmistress would not sit and watch her daughter kneeling on the ground waiting for whatever life was about to through at her. She joined her daughter in rolling in the mud begging the Lord's servant to soften his stance. The husband loved the wife too much to refuse her of anything, he agreed for the sinner to sleep in the house for the night until a permanent solution could be found the following day. Tilda left.

Unlike the first time, she had the courtesy of leaving a note explaining that she had been called back to work and she would come back in few days to see her son. Few days turned into few weeks and my parents were already planning to go to the city and dump the little brat wherever its mother was participating in promiscuous behaviour. Before they could pack it off, they took a final look at the boy. Although he wore oversized khaki shorts and no shoes, it was apparent that he was the fragile type, so thin that he would shatter if squeezed too hard. His well patched and even torn shirt exposed his smooth and handsomely dark skin. That was his only clothes. His huge black hair added an inch to his short height. His tiny nose and ears matching his small mouth with an adorable huge smile. And his eyes, sometimes I wonder if they only kept him because of his eyes.

At six Takura had neither seen the comeliness of moon nor the horror or the summer sun. His eyes could open but all what he has endured since birth was darkness. Unlike some children of his age, colours were a myth to him and the beauty of the night sky a legend to his pretty little ears. Takura's mother had never said anything about his blindness, she had just pretended that everything was well, but I knew my sister, it must have been tiring to ignore the difference.

The first thing I ever gave him was a walking stick. I picked up a perfectly straight wooden stick along the road, tied a tiny steel metal on one end and some cloth on the other end to make a comfortable handle. I didn't know if it was of any use but every blind person, I ever saw seemed to possess it. Later I was glad I did, after some few weeks of practice he was able to travel a bit further from our house. Without the need to crawl or kneel after few steps the stick gave him a huge smile and a little freedom.

The little freedom of walk allowed him to go and look for friends further than our homestead. This is how he discovered the other use of the stick, assaulting his mates. Believe me when I say he wasn't a bully he only beat up those who used to laugh or mock him about his eyesight. I was proud of him, at first, but it later turned out that he was really a bully. Once or twice every other week, an adult from the village would come to complain to the pastor about his grandson's hitting their child. It became a norm that caused the grandfather to specifically ask me to take away the stick from Takura.

No, I told the grandfather, Takura needs the stick to walk and defend himself out there it's a cruel world for boys like him.

The pastor did not understand, he believed in holy love. He wanted Takura to take everything in because his rewards and blessings were heavenly. He tried to teach him about love and doing good to your neighbour, but it was already too late.

Takura and I used to stroll around the village together a lot that people started to believe he was my son. I encouraged them; I didn't find any fault in it. It didn't sound strange when he started calling me father, although for a while I had to explain repeatedly to my then girlfriends the existence of this motherless child. The sight of us walking hand in hand was so touching that some villagers offered us some coins. We took them bought ourselves some sweets, we didn't need their pity, little acknowledgement that Takura was like another child was enough.

He was like other children, Takura was. In our happy hours I used to teach him to whistle and play a drum. He was way better at singing and dancing than me I later learnt. He was afraid of water and I had to give up teaching him swimming because he couldn't let go off my hands when we were in the water. It wouldn't come as a surprise that ploughing and herding cattle wasn't easy for him but shearing nuts, packing, and storing maize was something the entire family left him to take care of on his own.

My mother wanted me to teach him how to play music, that way when he was old enough, he would make noises and tunes in streets and buses to warranty handouts from strangers. If I had been holier then I would have just prayed for a better future for him. My mother was kind enough to teach him to wash his own clothes, I do believe she did it so that she could not touch the filthy blind bastard's underwear. I don't even know if my father acknowledged his presence at his homestead. Tilda never asked about him and I am glad he never asked of his mother too, I want to believe that he saw in me an uncle worth be a father. A kind family he deserved.

It has been two years since I last saw the boy. My father, the dear old pastor, sold one of his prized cows to send Takura to the special school that cater for his needs. The school is in the city and I can't afford to visit him. I couldn't tell if it was out of love or the desire to get rid of the bastard that drove my father to do such selfless act, but I am glad he did. Now I can hope that there is a future and place for him in the society we live in. Despite being in the same city with his mother they have never met or talked since he was six. We regularly send each other letters, although his have become less frequent than ever. He will find a person kind enough to read and write his letters, Takura claims. It doesn't matter, I always tell him, you will always have a special place in my life.

THE DEMOLITION
HOSEA TOKWE

The Commuter Bus did not stop at the popular DST Bus Stop but moved on into the City. There were groans and howls as the few passengers who had "*Pass Letters*" complained to the driver. These were the lucky ones to be allowed to board the bus and enter the City during this time of the Coronavirus pandemic outbreak. The bus had stopped at a manned roadblock some two kilometres away and the traffic police were satisfied with the evidence they were shown. Indeed these passengers had genuine reasons to come into the City.

"Where are you going to drop us now huh?"

"Hey stop here!"

"This old man is a deaf idiot" bellowed a bulky man furiously.

But the old metallic bus with its loud deafening engine moved on. The rattling noise from the old engine drowned out all else and some women who were already enjoying the spectacle laughed amid the confusion. Passengers who had left their seats intending to drop off at the popular bus stop stood along the aisle but the bus moved on. Now it was weaving its way through the fast built-up of traffic as workers eager to be at work early competed with each other amid the heavy hustle and bustle.

Jealous, a tall middle aged man, putting on a black cap inscribed "*New York*" on the forehead wore a dejected look on his face and sat pensively by the seat close to the door anxiously watching the aged bus driver dressed in a faded green shirt with threads on seams as he struggled with the handbrakes. Sharp knuckles shown on the driver's right hand and dark thick veins bulged as he summoned all his effort to control the rickety bus that heaved and jerked each time it pulled off as the traffic jam eased.

"I will drop here conductor" announced a middle aged man

"Noooo!" responded the conductor

"You will get me arrested for jumping at a traffic intersection from a moving bus" he shouted with a voice full of anger.

Now he was reminding every passenger that they had travelled very well all the way from the locations and now that they were weaving their way in the city he did not want any trouble with the police. But the passengers were restless shoving each other but he could not allow them take it their way until arrival at the bus rank, the final destination. The passengers were growing restless as the commuter bus was now taking too long to arrive as it negotiated the clogged traffic.

Tired of standing Jealous sat down again and gazed through the window at the old building "*Victory Building 1953*". This is the building that had been turned into one of the thriving *Nyaningwe Supermarket* in years gone by now. It has been one of the Supermarkets that had accepted multicurrency purchase of goods soon after the formation of the Government of National Unity (GNU) but to imagine it being closed now was difficult to fathom.

Something unusual caught Jealous' eyes. Where were the vendors who by now would have been unzipping their huge sacks of merchandise and laid them on the city pavements? Again he was asking himself why the foreign currency dealers' cars with dark-tainted windows were not at their parking lot. He felt a slight apprehension.

"Tickets tickets tickets please" the smiling conductor extended his arm to receive back half torn tickets. The bus had now arrived at the deserted old rank.

Jealous stood up and stepped into the aisle as he took a breather whilst the other passengers trickled out in single file. Soon he dropped his right foot to the ground he felt some cool air. There was a deadly silence and a cool wind was moaning softly through what used to be a busy and noisy terminus. As it blew from the east it swept some scrap papers in all directions. Jealous found himself wiping away dust from his eyes. The bus rank was deserted and bus sheds were bare and empty. Was he at the right place? At first he could not believe his eyes.

"Hit it hit it" an uproarious bunch of unemployed men urged on.

"Damage it, destroy", bellowed another man

Jealous moved faster urged by the spectacle from the crowd. Men, women and vagrants milled as they cheered wildly at the noisy Cat Demolition Caterpillar vehicle. As he urged closer he could now see its sharp claws twisting and turning in the air as if looking for prey. The driver reversed the monster like Caterpillar and it advanced forward amid wild cheers, its target a lone pillar.

With a forceful strength it hit the pillar. The pillar at first stood its ground shaking sideways buoyed by steel rails that had held the cement for years, but then its resistance would not hold forever and it dropped off heavily leaving a cloud of dust in the air. It was reduced, a heap of rubble.

"What is happening?" Jealous heaved with astonishment.

Nobody answered him at first

"I said what is going on here?" Before he could say out another question a man with dusty hair nudged and cupped his mouth to his ears.

"This is the demolition" he hissed into his ears

"The Municipality is demolishing all illegal shacks that had been erected here at the bus terminus all these years" giggled the man as he watched the crowd cheer again at another falling pillar.

Three weeks in advance word had gone that the Municipal authorities were going to pull down all the sheds and shacks that had sprouted at the popular Kudzanayi Bus Terminus. This terminus had been built before Independence for rural bus operators to pick and drop passengers. With the turn of the century and the economy worsening from 2005-2008 vendors had erected more stalls, some selling their merchandise in the form of nails, hoes, shovels even yokes and fencing wire. From another end where the Omnibus picked up passengers commuting from high density suburbs, where the majority of low income earners lived, vegetable, fruit and tomato stalls soon sprouted alarmingly. Then the small groceries mini-shops mushroomed, here the "poor man's shops" as they became known became very popular selling their basic commodities like cooking oil, sugar, soap and salt in the much detested Zimbabwe bond notes currency. It was said one could get any product in these mini shops. With the sudden emergence of the Coronavirus threat the local city fathers could have none of it. The Mayor of the City of Gweru had been in the news announcing that all these shacks would be destroyed in order to bring back sanity to the City and enforce strict City By-Laws. It had been overheard that some of the Municipal Officers were running clandestine stalls using middlemen to run their illegal informal businesses. This brought more urgency for the speedy destruction of the stalls to avoid prosecution.

Jealous had come into the City of Gweru, the City of Progress so they called it those days. Staying with his Uncle in the high density suburbs Jealous soon applied for an Engineering Certificate Course at the local Polytechnic and commuted daily. Bright, brilliant and intelligent, Jealous was already making plans for his future. With so many industries in the light industrial areas he was certain he would secure a job after finishing his course. Two years had passed and Jealous achieved his dream, a Certificate in Engineering.

"Now what would you like to do now" Jealous' father threw the question which caught him unawares.

"I will get a good job and after a year will plan to further my studies at any University in the country" responded Jealous with a broad smile on his face.

His father now aging, disagreed and advised him to get married for life in the city was not safe for a working young man, he told him. He did not want to disappoint his aging father, so he got married. Back in the City Jealous stayed with his Uncle.

Uncle Jethro was a Municipal Police Sergeant then. His work involved supervising street raids. Despite vendors being allocated stalls others had resorted to laying their wares on street corners beckoning passers-by to buy their wares. This practice annoyed Jealous for at some street corners there was disruption of free movement. Uncle had at one point invited Jealous to apply for a job but he was quick to turn back the advice. To imagine him an Engineering Certificate holder chasing after women vendors was an affront to his qualification. He had even hinted about his uncle's advice to his friend who had secured a University place who quickly advised him against it. But Uncle Jethro had insisted on him getting employed and support his family for going to University he said, would be like signing a death certificate. He alleged that University students had become drug pedlars, misfits of society and of lose morals by cohabiting in University Hostels. He even told him that others had turned into gays and lesbians. Jealous did not give mind to all this talk for his focus remained on furthering his education.

That was two years ago, Jealous as he wore a faded green shirt had realised that all his dreams had been shattered. The economic meltdown came at the turn of the century as Zimbabwe experienced a hyperinflation never seen in the country's history. Left with no option he teamed up with friends, secured a passport and found himself travelling and crossing borders into Botswana, a foreign land to buy groceries for resale at home. It worked as Weekend Street Markets were opened. Things worked well for sometime but as things turned everything came to an end. The short-lived experience had taught Jealous a valuable lesson in survival.

The economy never improved. Could he still stay at home and only wait to be fed by his Uncle? No! Jealous shook his head as he remembered when he had managed to buy food for his family, feed his aged father and even clothing his sightless granny. Now each day Jealous would wake up and visit the produce market. He would find the market full of tired and sweating people moving with little effort and speaking in low voices as if to conserve energy. Here and there week long banana leaves and yellow buns could be seen in open baskets where they were now cracking under the cruel sun. Tobacco leaves dangled from strings like dead rats.

The people milling about at the market were drowsy, as though the burning rays had melted their strength and resolution. Even insects, which always fluttered and buzzed about happily in the mornings, the light gleaming brightly on their wings, had now disappeared into the shadows. Life was hush, people were hustling and the bus terminus had been turned into a sprawling marketplace of heterogeneous products. Amid this entire melee, there were basket-weavers and storytellers and petty thieves and brigands in abundance.

Now all this was gone. Jealous had heard his Uncle talk about the demolition, but then the Lockdown was already being enforced.

As he stood visibly disoriented, he could not believe that right where he stood was the exact location where a thriving business was once conducted. He tried in vain to reconstruct in his mind the details of the stall he had owned. Why had he not listened to words doing the rounds about news of the demolitions assuming they were mere rumours. Of course the City Fathers no longer wanted informal traders to do their business in the Central Business District.

Jealous stood there confused. As thoughts raced through his mind, two big teardrops slipped out of his eyes and rolled unheeded down his cheeks. Inside him the world had crashed and his body felt heavy.

"Hey move away, move away" the Municipal Sergeant accompanied by his team had jumped from a pick-up as police details moved a distance away.

"We said we no longer want people, but you keep on coming"

"Move away!!" he shouted angrily

"Go to your rural homes and cultivate crops"

"Don't you have rural homes" another Municipal Policeman mocked

"And you young man! You are an embarrassment standing as if you have nothing to do"

"I said move before I bushwhack you" the Municipal Sergeant warned.

The humiliation that Jealous felt gnawed his heart. The harder he tried to push it to the back of his mind the more it tortured him. He was hurt and the cut was very deep in his soul. His youthful face had become like that of an old wizard approaching his eighties. Weighty considerations now occupied his mind.

The sun rose announcing that soon it would be hot. The demolition continued as the roaring sounds of the Caterpillar deafened the environs. The crowd some fearing arrest soon dispersed one by one. Their feet negotiated their way through rubble, big concrete slabs, contorted metal poles and remnants of broken planks and black plastics that had provided the shed to their wares. Built in the early twentieth century the Rural Terminus was at last gone, Gweru the *City of Progress* had regressed into an abrupt quietude.

As Jealous looked at the demolition for the last time, an overwhelming worm of despair and sense of irredeemable loss wriggled in the very marrow of his bones and was slowly eating him away as he retraced his steps home.

Raki
Takunda Shepherd Chikomo

I'm not saying I'm a lucky bastard but on this particular day I felt like one. That "lucky enough ndapona" Oliver Mtukudzi song since that moment became more than just a song to me, it became an anthem. I found my atonement on this fateful day.

My car is an old piece of metal, being an heirloom it has seen its fair share of near misses. I was taking the final stretch of Chitungwiza road before I took the right turn into Tilcor road, which would be my last stretch of tarred road before the dust one that would lead me straight home.

So I pressed on the gas and pushed the needle up to 120. Even I could feel that the machine was stretching its legs more than it should because it then grew an unusual vibration to it and the engine noise at somewhere around eighty kilometres per hour changed from a hummy groan to a robust grinding noise that made it feel like it was speeding when it wasn't.

Regardless, I pressed on, ignored my wife who by the time I got to 120 had woken up from her travel sleep and I could see by the boogie look in her eyes that these palpitatious bulging of eyes wasn't just her waking up from sleep but she was warning me that I was speeding and had to reduce speed. In my defence I was tired and besides it was the last stretch of road before getting home, what could possibly go wrong? So I hit it even harder.

Of course it was a wide tarred carriageway, I wasn't speeding that much, my car of inheritance was just scared of anything above a hundred, well, I wasn't. Besides I wasn't even going that fast because there were some powerful 21st century beasts that were still being hit where blood oozes such as the Mercedes C220 that passed me and the Prado VX Executive that looked as though they were being driven by some honourable ministers who were rushing to parliament to commit some honourable crime.

Nonetheless, this wasn't reason to hate my 84 Toyota Cressida because it still went fast enough to scare my wife in the front passenger seat, and myself too. Inside lane, approaching at 120 kilometres an hour, came my white Cressida, right indicator now on, I knew it to notoriously fail whenever it pleased so I also made a hand signal, my right hand out, pointing right in an up and down motion, I signalled thrice and began to ease off on the gas. I could hear the two litre diesel engine begin to breath and moan much peacefully as I let go off the gas for the brakes.

Chitungwiza road is intersect with Tilcor road which to the other end then leads to Chitungwiza's once vibrant pride and joy, Tilcor industrial area. Now it's just a ghostly scrapyard where the only sign of life is the tortured Zupco bus company depot and the residential dump site that's cleaner than our houses because the Municipality dare not collect waste anymore. This being the norm in Chitungwiza, we make do without traffic lights. "...drivers are to drive at their own risk and practice safety..." I once heard a VID officer say this to a colleague of his at Makoni VID. Today his words were put to the test.

Flying like the concord, to my left, a car overtook my Cressida in the blink of an eye. It went so fast what was left of it was just the sound of a car that had already passed. It was a grey Volkswagen golf MK7. He took me just as I was taking my right. In the opposite lane there was approaching a white Nissan Tiida that was signalling to turn right, thus was going in my opposite to the Industrial area. This Tiida driver assuming he had evaded danger by avoiding the large pothole that lay proud in the middle of road right by the intersection, nothing in the world was to prepare him for what was going to happen next.

That's when it all happened. The Volkswagen took me as I turned right, the Tiida turned also, so that meant there's no way the driver could have seen the golf coming and also manoeuvre around the pothole in time to successfully evade the golf, so he just made for it. In that moment, tyre screeches sounded so heavy and loud it felt like the car was going to burn them out in that instant. The driver of the golf seeing the Tiida approaching into his lane, dashed to the left, hit his brakes hard and in that instant the world took a chill pill and everything in that one second happened in slow motion.

As the Tiida driver came to his senses in that New Yorkian time he too hit his brakes hard, stopped, held onto his steering wheel for dear life, his mind possibly assuming what could have been the worst because had he stopped half a second late he could have been involved. The grey Golf was still in motion, swerving to the left and then right leaving a trail of dark smoky S's in the tarmac.

What I should mention is that this intersection is also where mini buses from Makoni to Machipisa drop off workers and pick up other passengers, so it's quite a buzz as people and cars play real life Monopoly. The grey car as it tried to evade the Nissan swerved left, where there were a group of workers waiting to hitch a ride back home after a long working day. One man of about his early thirties, he's the one who said, "Mukabika sarai muchidya mega".

The golf picked him up by cutting off both his legs, making him airborne, hit his back hard against the frangible windscreen smashed it inside, got stuck in there as the driver made a dash for the other direction to avoid hitting other people and he just lay there motionless and lifeless. Since his car was moving so fast he couldn't stop in time to avoid an eighteen wheeler Scania truck that was oncoming in the opposite direction. The grey car, with the industrial worker on screen crushed into the truck head-on, blood spilling all over, like raspberry juice. By the roadside people were just standing akimbo mouths open wide, others who had the strength had hands on the back of their heads and some covering their wide open eyes and mouths. Those who had been missed by the swerving car ran for their lives and jumped into the nearby grassy bushes and watched from there. Some later on confessed to wetting their pants.

He smashed right into the haulage truck, and in that moment his car blew up into flames, the fire erupting like the Hiroshima Nagasaki, and the noise there was so intense it surely felt like a bomb had gone off and deafened our ears. Because HGV's are not that quick to stop, the truck dragged with it the grey car, smashed it into the back of the Nissan Tiida which was still by the middle of the road, rolled it over three times and it too caught fire and lit up in flames beyond recognition.

As the truck finally came to a halt, other drivers who had witnessed this carnage, quickly ran to the grey Volkswagen that was glued in the face of the truck and burning and poured fire extinguishing fluid into the face of the fire trying their best to cut it out. When they eventually did, it was too late to have any hopes of saving a soul from the wreckage. The unfortunate industrial worker was charred by the fire, two occupants in the front, including the driver were crushed into their seats, half burnt half butchered by the front bumper of the truck because it smashed right into the windscreen, through the already knocked out man into their half bamboozled limbs and leaving them there just like that. As if they didn't have any life just a few seconds earlier.

The truck driver having suffered severe head injuries couldn't move out of his truck, so I made for the door and made my best to open the stuck door and help him out. Because the door was jammed, I smashed the window, got inside the truck, called for assistance and helped the helpless man out. Meanwhile another man was already making emergency calls to the hospital and fire brigade, because in that moment that's when the truck driver said diesel and pointed out to a large 1203 tank he was carrying behind. It had not occurred to us that his truck was ferrying diesel to a station at Makoni. I recalled earlier passing by the station and there was a long winding queue of cars, buses and trucks alike. Having been made aware of this highly flammable situation, there wasn't any time to waste because the tank had already begun leaking. An alarm was raised and people quickly moved to a safe distance from the scene.

Thirty minutes passed, the grey car had reignited itself, spreading the fire to the head of the truck which in turn ignited the diesel tank that exploded even bigger than had happened earlier. The earth shook with the force of nuclear bombs, causing the women who were by the scene to wail and constipate their faces into what only could be described as a frenzy of cries. Although safe in a distance, the heat was so intense people's faces could be seen sweating in the orange light. The fire guzzled into the sky lighting up the dusky evening as though the sun had lit up the earth the second time, only that this time around the light was more pronounced than a lazy dusky sun about to knock off into its mother's baby pouch.

The fire response team was nowhere in sight, besides their station being a five minute drive from the scene of the accident. I guessed they didn't have water in their fire trucks. The ambulance only came in time to pick up the corpse of the truck driver, they too were true to their promise of showing up…not to save a soul but to carry a dead one, if you're lucky they will carry one alive only for them to be pronounced dead by the time they get to hospital. Chitungwiza general wasn't that far away either, they must have been late because they were waiting for fuel, probably the same fuel that now lit up the night sky.

We just stood there, helpless…

(Raki - a loose direct translation in Shona of the English term lucky).

78

The crusade

Oscar Gwiriri

A Good News Bible was in Chamunorwa's left hand whilst the right one sporadically clenched into fists as if it was activating his mind to concentrate on what was in his thoughts. He felt as if his face was peeling off with the Honde Valley heat.

'The church must do something about upgrading the road to my homestead,' he thought. His imagination of being Jesus toiling up Golgotha kept him going up the hill. He arrived near a kraal and remembered how he used to spend so much time there watching a dung beetle pushing a ball backwards. However, he also recalled and regretted the boyhood games and all the 'wasted years' he lived in the village wrapped in ignorance of true worship. He condemned his past participation in traditional 'devilish' rituals. His pace dropped as he recalled the day elders and his peers laughed at him after failing a masculine exercise at the traditional initiation shrine. He had received the manhood lessons, then on the final tests each of them was tied on the waist with a yoke strap to practice an erotic dance. Thereafter they got circumcised. During that initiation, Chamunorwa released his bowl. The village elders called him a 'woman' and many predicted an ill fate on his reed mat.

Solo who was seated with the elders at the courtyard was not impressed by his cousin Chamunorwa whom the elders were giving a home-coming and merry reception. Their grandmother brought a clay pot of the seven-days-brewed beer, which was due for sale the following day, Saturday. Saturday was an appropriate day for guzzling.

Suddenly, a village juvenile ran into the courtyard panting and shouting, "There are intruders down the valley! Maybe war has started again! Intruders, invaders down there pitching up tents! Tents bigger than this courtyard! Bigger than grandmother's kitchen hut!"

"What! Never in my territory! Warriors, check it up then beat up the *Shima* drum to gather the village men if all is not well! Never!" The chief, Solo and Chamunorwa's grandfather fumed.

By then Solo had not yet greeted Chamunorwa who was sitted on a chair which belonged to the chief's aides. A suit swallowed him and a necktie was pulled loose on the neck.

"Take it easy grandpa; I came along with those people. They are under my command." Chamunorwa reassured.

"That's what you should have said first upon your arrival Chamunorwa, lest we harass visitors and disappoint the ancestors."

"I was about to do so grandpa" Chamunorwa defended.

"You children really don't grow. First thing first! Why then did you abandon them down the valley? Your grandmother brewed beer as if she predicted that there would be visitors. Anyway, she should have got the prediction from a bee which was buzzing around her." Grandfather smiled.

"Not really grandpa, they don't drink. They are devoted Christians. Original and genuine!" Chamunorwa emphasised.

"The village is full of church goers. We're Christians too." Grandfather swiveled a beer calabash and continued to say, "We still go for Sunday service at our Holy Cross Manunure Church."

Twang! Twang! Twang! The sharp ringing sound of crashing guitars echoes from the caves, disturbing an interesting conversation. Skeletons of chiefs falling on each other rattled in the nearby sacred Bura caves. Down the valley, a diesel generator groaned, but the groan was gulped by the 1-2-3- testing of the haunting high-output metallic distorted tones of seven-string guitars. Confusion set in as the elders glanced at each other's face searching for an answer for no question. Chamunorwa explained about his arrangement to have a Ministry at the village.

"Whom did you arrange with first of all? Don't you know that you may disappoint the spirits of the soil? You children never learnt

80

enough during your youthhood lessons and practices." Grandfather asked.

Grandfather was angry with all of the youngsters as he was seated over there scrutinising Chamunorwa.

'Chamunorwa is still a mosquito thin. All what he seems to have acquired from the city is the forced dignity and some somewhat new clothes. Oh, ancestors have mercy.' Grandfather thought.

'No matter how Chamunorwa undermines our traditional values, the elders seem to compromise, and above all they are giving him undue respect. But why?" Solo thought.

His rational mind raged again, 'After all, who is he to sit on our chair of authority? Chamunorwa, the mere boy who failed the traditional test and further failed at school, then resolvedly joined the church to compensate his weaknesses? Why is the church treated as a refuge institution by those with social shortcomings?'

Solo's eyes screwed on Chamunorwa's dressing whilst the elders were forging the way forward with the church crusade in the village valley. A lump of saliva choked Solo's throat. He quitted the traditional court session in silent protest.

Solo walked round the village searching for his friends. Nobody was home. Absolutely nobody. Livestock had been already closed behind pens, yet it was not yet eve. The praise and worship down the valley was sweet and luring. Solo swore to himself that he would never go there. 'After all the elders never bothered to consult us as usual as *the future of the village* as they have always promised.' Solo condemned the traditional courtyard discussions. He thought, 'How could Chamunorwa casually greet me as if I had not lost a mother during his absence? Not even a word or face of condolences? I hate him for this cultural misnomer. But how come, not even a lamentation offering' Solo was perplexed.

Solo complained to himself as he was walking down the valley where the arrows of the musical instruments, praise and worship and mourning were escaping through the big tent side folds. Solo trickled on a stump. He was just wandering in the forest nodding his head time and again, pre-occupied with mixed thoughts. He found himself standing just a short distance from the crusade tent. It was demonically big. Big like crocheting acacia branches in the savanna. It had blue and yellow strips. So colourful even in that darkness of the eve. The canvas was rolled quarter way up like a school girl's socks. The tent lights powered by the noisy generator illuminated the black feet underneath the tent. Some were clean and others soiled. Bare little feet were in there too. Wrinkled and cracked thin legs stood still like steel rail poles erected in the ground. He could see shorts, culottes, dungarees, spray-on jeans and cropped pants balancing on high-heeled shoes swaying sideways. Dirt legs were thriving to imitate the modern dances. It was like a crop field infested with weeds.

'I will not enter into that tent. I hate it. My traditional beliefs and culture reservations restrains me. I'm not a cultural extremist of course, but principled.' Solo vowed to himself.

Solo somehow got angry with himself for coming closer to the tent. He involuntarily tapped his leg to the heavy beat and soft melodies, whilst listening to Chamunorwa who was giving preaching bouts. Solo raised his hands and plugged his ears with his forefingers for a while. Total silence and ancient peace surrounded him. He felt the ground cracking with sound. A multitude of feet were stumping it like the devil compressing corpses in a hell oven. The raucous guitars were stashing through the grains of his fingerprints just to pierce his eardrums. He could feel the atmosphere seemingly bewitched. He supposed that all the fresh air was suctioned into the tent leaving nothing for anything outside it. In his eyes he could see aggrieved village ancestral spirits perspired fire in an invasion protest. He felt that the masquerading mosquitoes were also scared of the so-called Chamunorwa's Ministry crusade. He could hear them flying away and bursting in the air. He turned his head and felt that the ancient spirits were threatened by the public address system, and ghosts resurrected from their graves then roamed around the grave yard. Yes, he could see the spectre sparks right before his eyes. He was convinced that something uncultured was happening inside the tent. Something his father never did even during the sacrament at Holy Cross Manunure Church. He wanted to walk away from that tent, but the music was enchantingly hypnotising. It was rather hysterical and luring.

Solo stood at the corner inside the holy tent. Village children were dancing their hearts out, and swirling sweets had been thrown in the air. Village elders folded their arms at breast level, gazing. Grandfather was just standing there in astonishment like everybody else. The strangers were really rocking. Rocking madly. Praise and worship dominated even the village dogs' barking and owls' hooting. Testimonials time and sermons time came and passed by. The electric band was playing on a rostrum behind Chamunorwa's glass podium. A lead guitar was thrilling and raising Solo's hair when played on its own. There were no benches like at Holy Cross Manunure Church. The praise and worship ladies had their hair strengthened, some curled, and others were in black-eyed songbird's style. They had long stretched short and body tops, which shaped all the contours of their holy bodies.

'Attractive and arousing girls. Chamunorwa must be having a nice time with them I think. Had it been me, with all those beautiful girls? Oh shame, poor Chamunorwa is a 'woman' after all.' Solo thought.

There were a few adult strangers in the tent. They were also dressed like the youths, and above all, they were with the women not putting on head shawls like the village women ought to do. They also sung, shouted and cried in tandem with the hysterical youths. Most of the visiting ladies were dressed like young girls, but seemed to have clocked past the age of marriage like Chamunorwa.

Chamunorwa bellowed his sermon in English whilst stubbornly lodging his left hand in the trousers pocket and his right hand like a madman begging to some berated spirits. Another Brother translated it into standard Zezuru. The villagers were an ancient Manyika tribe, and some of his words did not go down well with them. Foul language some sort of swirled and swelled beneath the tent like a tornado.

Chamunorwa grovelingly broke into song:
Humble ya Salf
Before da Lawdy ...
His peers shouted above their souls:
He-will-lift ya up!
Chamunorwa continued, tears trenching down his bony cheeks,
He will lift ya-aaah!
'Tears? Oh, silly boy! Poor Chamunorwa. What a shameful bunch of a foible.' Solo uttered.
Chamunorwa continued and repeated the chorus whilst facing up the tent as if luring for a drop of water from the sky spirits.
He will lift ya up!
The guests were also raising their arms high above their heads imitating everything Chamunorwa was doing.
'Shame! Anyway, it's not bad for a 'woman' to lead other women and stray men.' Solo thought.

The crusaders exploded into prayer. Cried their guts out. They hopped and shouted. Hands clapping and waving became the order of the prayer. Chamunorwa concluded his prayer and his followers automatically halted in a certain fashion. The villagers watched with awe. The Sisters wiped sweat off their powdered brows. The Brothers' shirts were wet with salty sweat. The villagers were perturbed by the revival, compassionate dragging and soulful singing by Chamunorwa and his praise and worship Brothers and Sisters

Blessed assurance, Jizas is mine:
O what a fore taste of glory divine!

Chamunorwa's voice drowned into a horsy and trancing groan. Solo watched his grandfather nodding his head with amazement. The strangers clapped hands as they sang along:

This is my story, this is my song,
Praising my Saviour all the day long.

They repeated and repeated the chorus. A sister's soprano voice kept the song going lowly as Chamunorwa fell into a trance of prayer:

O Lawdy my Gawd! Lawdy my ...aah!
Punish those corrupt ... aah!
No matter judgment is for... aah!
But Gawd can't you see development is lagging in... aah!
Punish 'em if you're the real Gawd I... aah!
Cleanse this village of... aah!
Serve them from the vain orthodox worship... aah!

The strangers interjected with exclamations before the completion of each sentence:

Amen! ...Hallelujah!...Say it Bro!... That's it man!
Praise the Lord!... Jizas!... O my God! ... Save him!

Almost every visitor in the tent was closing eyes. Arms flung outwards. The worshippers burst into prayer once again. What a fracas atmosphere before Solo's scrutinising eyes?

The attending villager's in the tent failed to cope up with the pace of events in the beautiful canvas. Chamunorwa called sinners to the front for a collective repentance prayer. None of the villagers even lifted a foot.

'I don't want a 'woman' to set his hands on our sacred people.' Solo thought.

Chamunorwa shouted,
Come ye brothers and sisters!
Lawdy is watching and waiting!
I know this village is full of sinners.
Come! Have courage! Come!

The presumed village sinners stuck their feet on the suffering and trashed grass underneath the tent. All villagers knew that Grandmother Matondindo was a witchcraft queen. She didn't limp to the repentant front post.

'No matter we are lost sheep in the eyes of the crusading guests, we are alright as we are. It is fine being in the same blanket labelled as 'sinners' than having a faction of the righteous and us the 'thickheaded' hosts that will disintegrate our unity as a village people. I like it this way rather.' Solo thought.

"Anyone born of a woman repents every day. Brothers and sisters from Harare, come for prayer," Chamunorwa shouted.

The guests queued up, singing:

O, there is power, power
Wonder-working power!
In the blood of the Lamb!

Chamunorwa set his hand on each guest repentant's forehead, praying briefly. Some repentants spoke in tongues and others fell down as they were prayed on. The public address system was playing, and the keyboard was mesmerising the congregants. Grandfather pulled out his snuff horn, poured a little bit of it on his heel hand, pinched, sniffed and logged some in his mouth. A sing-a-long by the villagers dominated. Crescendo. The strangers were blessed once again.

One of the ladies offered a prayer, "God redeemer my! Surrender thyself unto you Lawd. Gwiriri village this in Lawdy. Bless sinners single souls every of non-repentant village Gawd. Thy shy come unto thee... Blaa...ta.ka.ma...takataka. Bizarre...Gawd" The lady spoke in weird tongues.

The other guests followed suit, speaking in tongues, in that beautiful tent. Stumping of shoes rocked the then bare ground. Cultic shouts and prayers engulfed the colourful tent. Solo watched in confusion. Oh, what a truly enigmatic worship!

The guest crusaders automatically stopped simultaneously to Chamunorwa like a lorry uphill force to an emergency halt.

That lady continued praying, "I know devil you no wait waylay villagers! Devil, take all property mine! Mine husband and everything, but my Jizus no! Gave me Jizus! Gave me Jizus! Gave me Jizus!"

The crusade swallowed the whole night. For surely, time is like dew under a leaf. The cocks crowed. A second and third cock crow followed suit.

Chamunorwa lined another prayer session, "Oh Lawdy, Gawdy my mercy! No matter my people can't repent, I will not deny you! Three times the cock has crowed, and I am steadfast, awake doing your work Lawdy. I can't deny like Jonah, this village is Nineveh. It's Israel, Sodom and Gomorrah. O, Lawdy... Gawdy....Gawdy! Rama...tapa..tipa...tapa!"

No matter the singers looked tired and sleepy, the instrumentalists kept on banging. A few Sisters still jingled their tambourines. Some villagers inclusive of Solo had missed their dinner. The strangers had their food packs behind the tent and they took turns to feed. The crusade embraced dawn and rewound with a dolce song:

Awake, my soul, and with the sun
Thy daily stage of duty run....
To pay thy morning sacrifice...

Solo also hummed to the tune. A Brother was walking around with a small artificial reed woven basket to collect offerings from the congregation. The villagers had no money anyway. One of them picked a pebble and placed in that basket. The Brother collected offerings from the strangers. The rays of the sun beamed on their feet.

Some strangers started packing bags, cutlery and instruments into their lorry. They left the keyboard player concluding the rejoicing. Chamunorwa once again called sinners to the repentant's post. Nobody turned up. His peers were then too busy packing up equipment.

Chamunorwa instructed the village youths to assist by picking up litter right round the place. Grandmother Matondindo approached him over what his peers had done when they arrived.

She complained, "Your girls climbed up my peach tree and they harvested all the fruits without my permission."

"Grandma, God created Eden. He did not give ownership of nature to individuals. God will provide and bless the tree with much more fruits during the next season. Believe me" Chamunorwa advised.

As the village youths were picking litter, one of the Brothers conversed with Solo.

"I am Chamunorwa's cousin brother." Solo told the Brother.

"You're blessed bro. Bro Chamunorwa is great, man! Blessed are you!" The Brother praised.

Solo felt honoured. Somehow, he began to like Chamunorwa. That Brother stood starring and admiring Solo as he kept himself busy picking empty food packs which were gathered at the corner of the tent.

"Throw that away! Drop it! Eish!" The Brother shouted pointing to the heap of rubbish grasped in Solo's hand.

"What did you say Brother?" Solo was lost.

The Brother looked aside. He never faced at Solo again.

"Drop that *Heart of a Man* pamphlet! There is a used condom in it!" He whispered to Solo.

"Used condom? I don't understand what you are talking about." Solo whispered back. He started separating the rubbish from his left hand with his right hand, throwing it one by one onto the ground so as to check what was all about the condom. Solo seemed he had never heard about it. The crusaders packed their stuff, and off they went back to the city.

'I will come back again. This time everyone must repent, voluntarily or by force' Chamunorwa thought.

The Big Boys' Club
Mildred Mutize

As usual, the gallery in High Court Number One where Judge Rickson Banga was presiding over the murder trial of Doctor Maxwell Pasi was fully packed. No one wanted to miss the reading of the final judgment that afternoon. Those who could not secure seats in the gallery resorted to TV screens and computers as the trial was being streamed live on broadcast. Everyone in the country hoped that the murderer will be given the harshest sentence for murdering a government minister in cold blood. What made people so furious was that Doctor Max, as he was affectionately known, was admitting to the charge yet proffering neither defence nor excuse for his heinous act. It was as if he had killed the minister for the love of it!

But as Judge Banga was about to begin reading out his carefully crafted judgment, something out of the ordinary had happened. There had been a caller on the telephone line who wished to be heard in the court immediately as his life depended on it. Everything he had learned in law school and in all the years he had been in this field told him that this was not possible, a witness had to appear physically in court and had to be sworn in. But as he opened his mouth, Judge Banga surprised everyone when he told the court orderly to put the call through. If the evidence was as inept as he suspected, he could as well choose to dismiss it, but he reasoned that there was no harm in listening to it. What came out through the external speakers had everyone completely stunned.

"I can say this is so mind blasting!" Judge Banga said when he finally found his voice. "Before making my judgment, I'll have to hear from both sides, state council?" he sighed, then sat back as the Public Prosecutor rose to his feet. He was a heavy looking fellow, slow in speech yet meticulous to detail.

"Your honour, this telephone conversation is a hoax meant to confuse the court and delay justice from being served. First of all, this witness has not been sworn in and if his life is actually in danger, he should have called the police and not this honourable court. Allow me to take you to the case of….."

The prosecutor rambled on but none of what he was saying reached to Judge Banga's mind. His senses were in turmoil. *They will kill me!* He thought wildly. The sharp contrast struck to him, of that time, five years ago when he had been the talk of the nation, when songs of praise had been sung for him. *It's the reason for my predicament now*, his mind told him as it glided back to that time.

The police officers in town had received numerous tip-offs over a new illegal drug which had invaded the streets and was being traded in secrecy. Fact had it that it was being manufactured in Kalibu, a country to the far north and was commonly known as the booster. The drug propelled and increased the number of neurons inside the brain cells, making people more intelligent, shrewder. If taken to excess, however, the neurons will keep on multiplying, forming lumps within brain cells leading to brain tumour. Quiet sadly, the drug had found a rampant and viable market in secondary schools, tertiary colleges and universities as many young students saw it as a catalyst to effective learning.

What perplexed the police was that of all the peddlers they managed to arrest on suspicions of supplying the booster, none among them budged any information regarding the source of the drug or the master minders behind it. What they only achieved to realise was the shocking truth that some primary school children were also now being sucked into the abyss. There was a sudden nationwide outcry as concerned teachers and parents demonstrated to the government for something to be done. But no matter the strategies the police employed, they could not crack the drug source within the country. All they knew was that it was manufactured in the Republic of Kalibu. Security at all the borders and airports had been triple tightened to guard against its smuggling into the country but still the peddling continued and hospitals became swamped with teenagers suffering from tumours.

One day, a suspect was nabbed at a local college gate by the intelligence police for drug peddling and was brought to court. Like many before him, he readily confessed to dealing with drugs but refused to reveal his source. Rickson Banga, a Public Prosecutor by then, after perusing the docket had asked the cops to let him talk to the accused. Naison Ndlovu was tall and lanky, with stained teeth and a foul breath.

There was an air of stubbornness around him.

Banga said, "Naison, it pains me to think you are going to spend the next twenty years in prison."

Naison guffawed insolently. "I'm prepared to go to jail for what I did."

Banga closed the docket and threw it aside. "Why am I even wasting my time? Of course you won't get convicted. The guys you work for will come and pay off the magistrate."

"They won't...!" He realised his mistake but it was too late.

A few minutes later, Banga was on the phone with the Officer in Charge Central Police Station. He gave him three names. Naison was now a key state witness, placed in a safe house with state security.

A week later, Ambassador Bothius Mare was recalled from the Republic of Kalibu where he had been assigned for the past ten years. He was arrested at the airport upon his arrival. He joined in the police cells, two well-known business tycoons, Regis Muto and Leeroy Mucha. They were being jointly charged of several counts under the Dangerous Drugs Act. The trio admitted to the charges. Their trial kicked off two days later with Prosecutor Banga leading the state's case. In the end, the three were found guilty and each sentenced to life imprisonment.

The news of the successful conviction of the leaders of the drug syndicate broke out and spread like a veld fire. The newspapers, broadcasts and social media were awash with the story and Prosecutor Rickson Banga was at the epic centre of praise. If Banga felt elated by the glory and applause on social media, a single phone call two days after the conviction brought him into euphoria.

"That was a job well done, Banga. You made us proud," the Area Prosecutor said.

"Thank you, madam." Banga grinned. Their boss was an iron lady who castigated more than she praised.

"The Governor called me," she went straight to the point. "He said he was impressed by your work and would like to see you this afternoon at his office. 2:15 sharp."

It was just unbelievable.

Banga was surprised by the faces he saw around the gold coated conference table in the grand office. The Governor, Joseph Gano introduced Banga to the men around. Banga was in the seventh sky as he shook hands with prominent men who, up to now he had only seen on television screens and newspapers. There were two government officials, three popular lawyers, about two Radio DJs, and a CEO of a giant company. Everyone in the room was well known in the country.

"Sit down, dear," Gano said. "You must be a real genius to be able to crack that one." All the men nodded.

"Thank you, sir. I was only doing my job." Banga said as he sat down.

"Your record as a senior prosecutor is very remarkable and hard workers should be rewarded. I've great news for you. The Prime Minister has appointed you judge of the High Court. Congratulations, Judge Rickson Banga!" They all clapped hands laughing gaily at Banga's surprised look.

One of the men handed Banga a card. "Here is your membership to the Big Boys' Club, where only important people meet and discuss crucial issues. You are now a member of the Club, Ricky! And one other thing, we are all boys here and we call each other by first name."

"And I'll be in charge of all your financial needs," Freddy, the CEO added. "Anything at all you want; a car, a house, you name it. A judge should be a cut above the rest."

Banga thought he would burst with joy. He felt like a young boy on his birthday, heaped present after present. If he had known the actual conversation between the Governor and the Prime Minister pertaining his promotion, he would have been more thankful to Gano. The Prime Minister had expressed shock when the Governor asked him to appoint Prosecutor Banga to a judge.

"Are you out of your mind, Governor!? Where on earth have you heard of a green eared prosecutor suddenly waking up as a High Court Judge?"

"Banga is not green eared, Sir. Just think of the good work he has done in solving that drug fiasco which has been giving us a headache. Surely promoting him to a judge is the least way we can show him our appreciation."

It had taken the Governor two other phone calls and a dinner with the Prime Minister before he reluctantly gave in to the request.

From that day, Banga's life changed for the better. After being sworn in, he was transferred to the High Court where he spent the first few months sitting in with other judges. He was a hard worker by nature and his in-depth knowledge of the law made him a resourceful person to fellow jury members and his superiors. In the legal circles there was a saying that a good law officer is not the one who knows the law but the one who knows where to find the law. Banga knew both and he was revered by many. In the evenings, he would hang out with the 'Boys' at the Club. Through the Big Boys' Club, Banga was now an acquaintance of the prosperous and important people in the country. All Club members were paid a handsome figure on weekly basis. They had standards to maintain, he had been told. His own standards had also risen and everywhere he went, people always turned to stare.

Banga had been a high court judge for five years when one day, he received an invitation to a formal dinner at a local hotel. As usual, he found himself rubbing shoulders with the VVIP who included foreign dignitaries, government ministers, and business tycoons, among others. Although the ambiance was formal and reserved, Banga could detect a degree of casualness among the guests who were so at ease with one another. He revelled in the fact that he was part of them.

"Got a minute, Ricky?" Gano was beside him, a glass of whiskey in hand. He led Banga out of the drawing room into a smaller office where the Boys were chatting idly, taking sips from their glasses. Gano closed the door as Banga exchanged casual greetings with the Boys before proceeding to the drinks corner. He poured himself a glass of whisky.

"You know, Ricky, you are doing us proud," Gano said behind him. "We like the way you preside over major cases."

"Thanks, Joe," Banga said, turning to him. The boys had all ceased their conversations and had come to stand in an arch behind Gano, facing Banga.

"We think it's high time you start the real work," Gano continued solemnly. "But of course ours won't be complicated. We have got a system where we grill our guys so that whoever is caught admits to all charges and never say a word on who is behind."

For a moment Banga was stupefied. "I…I don't understand."

Gano moved closer to him. "Look here, Ricky. We have got a business to protect. The proceeds are what take care of all of us in the Club. You see, that drug plant in Kalibu where the booster is manufactured is my brain child and the Club's cash cow. We have a large empire working under us that's why we are so rich."

Banga could see that all the Boys were eying him warily, watching closely his reaction. In that instant of deep shock, Banga saw something in the Boys that he had never seen in all these past years. Beneath the glamour they exuded, there was a deep lining of danger and it was surfacing now. He took a timid sip from his glass and when

95

he looked up, a huge grin covered his whole face. "Why did you guys wait this long to tell me? This is very exciting!" The Boys suddenly relaxed.

Gano looked happy. "I was telling the boys you won't give us any problems and they were doubtful. Do you know you were my project from the start? I'm glad you came out fine."

"Your project?"

Gano nodded. "Remember that time you made our peddler reveal some names to you? You gave us quite a fright then. We had two options; either to get rid of you and continue with our operations or to suspend our operations briefly and make you part of us for future use. All the boys voted for the former but I had a hope in you and how right I was! You are now mature enough to know the Club secrets. Peter, you can tell him about the drug fiasco."

Peter, a medical doctor said, "When we resumed our operations in this country last year, the borders were now too risky. We organised that the booster come in along with our country's medical drugs, so that no one suspect them. But things went wrong yesterday when our consignment arrived at the hospital's warehouse. I took along our peddlers to help with their conveyance to our place but as we were loading the truck, Doctor Maxwell Pasi, the Hospital Administrator arrived. Someone should have tipped him off and he in turn called the Minister and told him. He blocked our way and told us to wait until the minister arrives with the police. We immediately attacked him and he fell unconscious. I had to call Joe and he quickly organised someone to get to the minister fast before he spilled the beans."

Gano laughed and said, "You see, Ricky, our guy did an excellent job on the Minister last night and just so that the murder is not linked to our man, Doctor Max will claim responsibility. We pulled him through our processes and he came out fine, just like the rest before him. He is going to be arrested and he will admit to the murder charge." Gano placed a hand on Banga's shoulder and a cold, hard malice flashed in his eyes as he said quietly, "You are going to try him,

Ricky. I'll see to it that you do and you shall give him a death penalty." As Banga nodded, Gano had turned to Tasara, from the national broadcast. "I want the trial to be aired live. People would be interested to know that Doctor Max killed a government minister and whilst everyone is glued to the trial, we will smuggle in more drugs."

A week later, Doctor Max's trial had come to an end. That afternoon at 3:30, Judge Banga was going to read out the final judgment and sentence. At 2:45pm, Banga was knocking on the Judge President's chambers. He spent the next forty-five minutes with his boss, talking in confidence. When he finally got out, he headed straight to his courtroom, where everyone was waiting for him.

After the strange call which had everyone in the courtroom dumbfound, the Prosecutor had indeed taken his time, trying to persuade the court to disregard such evidence as there was a high chance of manipulation. When he finally took his seat, the Defence Attorney rose up and bowed low to the Judge. "Your Honour, I have nothing to say. I pray that you follow your instincts in this matter." And he sat down. Everyone was taken aback by this.

After a while, Judge Banga cleared his throat. "After having heard from both sides, I carefully weighed the odds and it is now apparent there is more to this case. I am now releasing Doctor Maxwell Pasi so that the police can make further investigations to this case." He pounded his gavel on the table, symbolising the end of the court session.

As the gallery stood up in anticipation of the Judge's departure, Banga raised a finger at the IT and media personnel who quickly folded their cameras and ran out of the courtroom. At that same moment, four uniformed police officers bowed at the door as they entered the court room. "Good afternoon, your Honour, we are here to offer you state protection."

In the Judge President's chambers the cameras were being quickly set. After a few seconds, Judge President Michael Dorgan was addressing the nation live on air. "Ladies and gentlemen, the situation has taken another twist. I would like to assure you that I've got the blessing of our government to say this on air as it concern the security of our country. This is about a very daring and dangerous drug syndicate which call itself the Big Boys' Club. As we speak the police have them under arrest. Let me start from the beginning...."

Mother's day
Oscar Gwiriri

I and Oswald, the famous writer were seated comfortably in the Comfort Lounge of Rock City Bar. It was decorated in celebration of the Mother's Day. Glittering ribbons were being blown by the chopper blade type of fan which was blowing out the smoke of the puffing cigars. The glitters illuminated like the motorcade flashes. They were somehow hypnotizing and giving a nostalgic feeling to some night owls.

"You see that wench over there, throwing eyes everywhere like an owl, that's what my mom was like during her youthhood." Oswald said whilst screwing his eyes.

"How do you know?" I asked.

"My aunts and other relatives told me" Oswald answered.

"Maybe just for you to hate her, she was not in good books with them, ha-a?"

"Man you'll never understand this, its queer to you, and you can't fit in my shoes, you see! You may think I'm drunk, but I'm as sober as a judge."

"And can't you mend the relationship then?" I asked.

"Can you ever mend the brains, man? I'm yet to be in such a brain surgery if it was ever invented, you see. I will never like mother! Never ever, ever! " Oswald swore.

Crash! An empty bottle which he had been mistakenly placed at the edge of the bar coffee table fell. It smashed on the tiled floor, but broke into a heart form and remained intact.

"Oh! Gosh! Possibly after a brain transplant, Man."

"Don't exaggerate your bitterness brother. With a little bit of some counselling, you will find yourself forgiving and loving her once again. Your mother is your mother. Lucky you, you still have one at such an old age as this."

99

"Little. I like that word, you see. What therapy do you talk about? Which counselling do you know, man? I have read all literature, short stories, poetry, novels, philosophy and listened to all music dedicated to mothers in search of my lost soul and the mother touch, and guess what, I yielded nothing out of it. Just pain and nothing else. Pain! Pain! Pain!"

Oswald shouted and shook his head, hitting his forehead with his hammer of the hand as if he wanted to shake out an irritating insect out of his skull.

"Is it not that you searched objectively? Offload your bitterness, and see the good side of your mother, brother. She carried you for nine good months, after all."

"No! It was only seven, imagine! Not nine, you see! Who knows, maybe I was on the way to the drains, and the spirits intervened. Hahaha!" Oswald threw a hysterically laughter.

He lit a cigar and pulled it quarter way like a monster. He held in the smoke as if he wanted it to diffuse into his entire body. After a long while, he puffed it towards the ceiling with his head raised in a sacrificial manner.

"For those who were dumped by their mothers!" He uttered. He pulled the cigar again half way, and puffed again with another utter, "For those thrown into dumpsites by their mothers!" He pulled once again to the extent that the fire got extinguished by the cigarette filter, and then he puffed again in the same direction, "For all girls following my mother's footpath."

He belched loudly. I wondered to whom he was really offering that sacrifice. Oswald was just a fine well kempt man. I wouldn't classify him amongst the schizophrenic writers I have read about. He was so smart, though a little bit dirt in his writing about women. My analysis detected that he was in denial with the fact that he had beef with his mother or women in general. I wondered if Oswald was really a drinker. I noticed that he took a sip once in a very long while. I even pondered why he frequented this bar to the extent that my friends had to advise me to check for him here than at home, for my intended interview. Maybe he was here for some observation or writing inspiration. Nobody knew. I was scared of asking him the reason why anyway. Ethics denied me digging too personal after all.

I observed that whenever Oswald left his chair, he went with his beer glass in hand, then returned with it empty. I chewed over whether he went to gulp it in the toilet or "*flash it in the drain*" as he thought his mother intended to do to him when he was born a premature baby.

Oswald seemed to be losing patience with my presence, possibly he wanted to jot some notes, I just don't know.

"Isn't your drink now hot, I can get you a cold one? Just summon the waiter." I broke the silence.

"Never mind, man. Too much alcohol is not good for your body, mind and soul. The only good thing to do in excess is writing. You write and write, then sleep, then wake up and write, and write, and write, and write, and write." His eyes shoot out as he spoke.

He wiped his lips and sniffed his right armpit. He pulled a small bottle of cologne and sprayed.

"But the educated say too much of everything is dangerous." I commented.

"Maybe, but not writing. Man, had I not been a writer pouring my tribulations on paper, boom, I could have gone to hell, you see!" He sipped a little beer and spit back into the glass.

"Why hell?" I asked.

"If your own damn mother dumped you, condemned you to the drains, how dare you expect heavens to accept you? This is not bar talk man, its reality, you see!" He answered care freely.

The club was lively, but there was somberness at the corner where we were seated. Oswald pulled out another cigar and clangs it between his head and the right ear. He started caressing the USB Electronic cigarette lighter.

"But I wonder why you still hang on to your past and your childhood after all." I initiated further discussion.

"The past is today. The past is tomorrow. The past is eternity." He whispered stammering and as if talking to himself whilst his eyes remained fixed on the glass of his beer.

"What do you mean?" I asked.

"Your soul is in your navel. If your umbilical chord was dried with red hot chilli like mine, somewhere, somehow the pain invades you subconsciously."

"So, when do you think you will feel that you have offloaded your bitterness completely on paper? I mean, when shall you halt demeaning women in your writings."

"A women activist, are you? Another bloody sponsored feminist?" He glowered.

I felt threatened, but had to persist for some reason.

"Not really, brother. I just mean, should we readers expect a happy theme from our celebrated writer or it is going to be mother-attack through and through?" I set a plastic smile.

"That's where you are lost, you see! I wonder where from do you critics get all that. Mother-attack! Which mother-attack? So, if one writes reality about a woman who never loved him, that's mother-attack? God forbid!" Oswald asked sardonically.

He stood up with a quarterly glass, and as usual walked to the toilet. Possibly he had to gulp it there or pour it in the urinal. It was almost forty five minutes since he had gone. I concluded he just went away without bidding farewell. I stood up and left too. Though I felt the offense of being relegated to a mere Rock City patron, I did not forget to pass through MoM's Confectionary to pick up my cake for a Happy Mother's Day.

Mourning and sunsets
Matthew K Chikono

Evening was already upon him as he made his way towards the village. He hadn't realised how time had glided past him, one moment the sun was mercilessly scalding his forehead and the next it was orange in colour snuggling comfortably into its mother's bosom. Tapera had walked the entire day and still had a long journey ahead of him before he could reach the village. The rumbling of his stomach reminded him that he had not eaten anything since the previous evening. Neither had a drop of water touched his lips. The tattered clothes he wore were now slowing his tired body down.

The events of the previous evening weighed heavily on his mind. Death and gore were all it had been all about. He still didn't believe that overnight his well-planned life and brightly lit future had crumbled down to dust. It was something Tapera had never imagined would ever happen to him. He had been on the verge of success. He would have been the richest man in town. They actually would have been the richest men in town, Tapera and Phiri.

The rumbling of the stomach came again, it wasn't hunger it was diarrhoea! Tapera quickly turned out of the well-trodden path and hid himself in the bushes. A sigh of relief escaped his mouth as he sprayed and drowned an entire colony of ants with his insides. Nothing was ever going to grow on that place again.

"Good evening to you."

A young woman, possibly not older than him, was passing through the road and greeted him. Tapera mumbled a reply. The woman continued her way but not before Tapera had noticed a thick layer of petroleum jelly pasted on her dark skin. The yellow dress she wore wasn't easy to miss and Tapera would have avoided such an embarrassment if he had looked careful enough before he had squatted and defecated beside the road.

In a minute or so Tapera was back on the road. He did not have enough time to dwell on his embarrassment, he had news of death to deliver. News of Phiri's death. Phiri had been a friend who turned brother and Tapera knew the news of his death had to reach Phiri's parents from him, not from strangers or the police. Phiri's family deserved to receive it from someone they knew.

Until this fateful day Tapera had always assumed that he could walk the thirty-five-kilometre trek between Pote river and Musana village in half a day. He had even tried to make a bet with Phiri a couple of weeks back when they left for the river, to mine gold. Gold-panners, that was what the government and other fancy people called them but the duo and the other hundreds of people digging in the pits didn't mind if they were called makorokoza. That's what they did, dig small pits along the river and pan tiny amounts of gold with mercury in a dish and sell to a buyer with ready cash. It wasn't legal but it brought the food on the table. It was the kind of job that made no one strong enough to walk long distances. Tapera thought so as he dragged his feet towards the remainder of the journey.

What Tapera could have killed for, as he walked, was a pint of cold beer. Cold millet beer like the one they bought when they came up from the pits. Some women sold it to them, expensive but worth every cent.

"So, you are drinking beer now?" Tapera's mother had asked when he had first come back home from work. He didn't find the need to explain himself, now that he was a man. If he earned the money, he had the right to buy whatever he wanted with it, even beer despite him being just seventeen. The boys he worked with, way younger than him, drank alcohol everyday like addicts and it was normal. Tapera tried to tell his family that but they didn't understand. They thought alcohol would be the death of him and Phiri. Alcohol hadn't been the death of Phiri, it was a bottle of water that led to his death.

104

Tapera reached the Supa growth point. It was heft with activity as expected of a Thursday evening. The seven dilapidated buildings served the community well despite three of them being bars and beer halls. The rest of the buildings served as grocery stores and a grain-miller. Tapera had grown up playing at the area, he knew every inch of the place. He also knew every person who happened to be selling their wares along the road. The regulars at the beerhall greeted him loudly. He could tell the news of the previous night had reached them and they were pretending to be oblivious so he could tell them the hot gossip. Tapera passed them with his head over his shoulders.

Chigwedere Sports bar stood with its inviting doors wide open. He would have been a fool not to accept its invitation. One too many times, Tapera had accompanied Phiri inside the building to drag out Phiri's intoxicated father and haul him home to his wife. Phiri's father was the benchmark of all the drunkards in the village, no one adored slavery to the ancient liquid than him. Most of the year, Phiri's father lay in a pool of his own vomit inside the beerhall and now the task had fallen upon Tapera to lift the old man up and drag him to his mourning wife.

A sigh of relief, loud enough to drown the loud music in the beerhall, escaped from Tapera's mouth as he entered the hall. Phiri's father wasn't amongst the horde of men who sat drowning their sorrows with alcohol, he was nowhere to be seem inside the beerhall. Tapera walked over to the counter, threw a couple of bills to the bartender, and pointed to a scud of beer. The bartender did not bother to check the minor's ID. The bartender with the money in hand gladly parted with the bottle of beer. The boy, with the beer in hand, went and sat on an empty bench. The loud music was just a whisper to the silence of his soul.

He took the first sip. It was in memory of Phiri who had been murdered with a shovel by a fellow panner. Phiri had taken a sip from the mukorokoza's water bottle without permission and the mukorokoza had retaliated with violence. He gulped half of the remaining contents of the beer. Tapera hadn't seen any of it, he had been busy looking for one of his shoelaces. Few seconds later he was at the door, with the holy blood coursing through his veins, determined to pass on the news of his friend's death.

The girl with the yellow dress stood at the door, hesitating to enter the hall. Tapera greeted the familiar face with a wide grin on his face.

The girl politely answered with a sly smile on her face. No, she wasn't a girl, she looked old enough to be Tapera's mother. She offered her services to the boy.

The boy looked out into the night, little stars were already dancing in the sky. It wouldn't do any good to bring news of death before supper.

Maybe he could wait a bit whilst he rested and convince the woman in the yellow dress that he didn't need her services. Surely Phiri could wait a bit, Tapera was already in mourning.

JOURNEY BY BUS TO CHITUNGWIZA
Nicole Kazembe

The September sun just above me, clearly stating it is summer time, SUMMER IS HERE, was so hot that l was walking with my arms a bit spaced so that air would pass through my armpits. Heavens knew how much l hated that round wet thing on clothes' armpits to show that you really are sweating. I was feeling relieved that l was now near the bus terminus, famously known as the Charge Office since it was located just next to the Police Charge Office. I headed straight for the buses which go to Chigovanyika but pass through St Marys'. They had signs written St Marys' then Chigovanyika on the bottom. I preferred the buses to the Kombis, anyway what average person wouldn't prefer these. It was all because they were cheaper at all times. Their fares were all the same throughout the year and all through each day. They cost fifty cent bond.

I boarded the bus and was the second passenger. I measured which side of the bus the sun will be hitting because l didn't want any sunburns on my forehead. Then I figured the sun will be hitting on the right side of the bus. On the left side of the bus I chose a seat by the window and as l sat l was so excited about the burger l had bought from Pick n Pay. It had been almost 2 months since l last ate a burger from there. I decided to first go on my WhatsApp and text back some few texts from my friend Linda. I had to update her if Kudzai, our other friend has answered her phone, she had not. I texted Linda that l would go to Kudzai's house the next day and check if she was ok. While I was texting, a man, maybe in his sixties passed me by. I am not sure about his age though because l am not the best at guessing people's ages. He was holding a plastic bag, containing a box of Chicken Inn and l don't know what else was in there but there was something else.

"We have to share that pie." The man said to me while passing then sat in the seat just behind mine. I only smiled. He had seen a tip of the paperbag the burger was wrapped in and it looked like the one from Baker's Inn, the ones they put their pies in so he quickly assumed it was a pie. "We have to share that pie my daughter", he repeated.

"Ok. We will share". This time I didn't do the smiling thing which I did often to make someone feel like I said something nice in a low voice but in actuality I had not. When I did this smile most people did not bother to say "Pardon" because obviously they didn't hear anything but just the warmth of thinking I responded to them kept them quiet. It was just a satisfying smile and I knew it. When this elderly man had said *daughter* I was so relieved because in my head most men who would start up a conversation would end up hitting on you. Most of these men would be old enough to be your grandfather. This elderly man looked old enough to be my father.

After I was finished with my texting, I removed my burger from the plastic bag and then packed the plastic bag in my handbag, I am not a fan of luggage. Now it was time for my burger. As I had my first bite, a beautiful and light in complexion woman with a small baby girl walked in. She had that proportional round nose, the ones I liked. Mine was round but a bit big in a way I did not like. Her brown eyes looked so innocent and had a distant sadness and emptiness but the weak smile of full lips and shyness covered these. She was from the Apostolic Church, the one where they wear complete white with bald heads. She sat on the right side of the bus just across from me, the side where the sun would hit her for the whole forty five minutes journey to Chitungwiza.

"Amai, huyai mugare ku side kuno kwebhazi. Ku side ikoko kunenge kuchirohwa nezuva nzira yese mwana angatsve". She shyly said Ok and started to gather her things, a little too slow for my liking. Was she still deliberating if she should listen to this man and move over to the right? She finally moved, to my relief of course. I now continued with my burger. From then on I did not notice how the bus

108

got full, there were even some standing passengers. The bus finally took off for Chitungwiza. I had finished my burger by then. I was glad the traffic was not bad at the time. It was not rush hour yet. We went on out of town. When we entered Seke road there were some people by the bus stop. So, the bus stopped and three people got in. There was some low grumbling from the already standing passengers but the bus driver still picked these three people. We went on. And when we came to another bus stop, that's when all hell broke loose. The grumbling was loud and the standing passengers were complaining. The passage was now full and there was not enough free space to go around. I heard a woman's voice talking back to the grumblers. It's actually a sight when a female becomes a bus conductor. They are there but it's a few of them.

At this second bus stop two people got in. I peered at the back of the passage to see if the passage was truly full. It was full and people were squeezed. I thought to myself if I got into a bus this full I would step out but people were determined to get where they were going on time. In this grumbling I remembered what the Zimbabwean people say when you travel in a car or bus and the people in it are quarrelling while it's in transit. They say you are likely to have an accident. I don't like accidents, I am sure no one else likes them too. In my heart I started praying my Hail Marys. I just say them in cases like these. When there is commotion around me and I can't seem to concentrate on prayer, I find it easy to concentrate on the Hail Mary. I did not want another accident. I had an accident earlier this year. I came out fine and everyone else involved in the accident. I only had some muscle tissue swelling which I got some rubs for. I have one finger though, on my right toe, the big one which I think was affected during the accident because every time I pour hot water on it, it feels like electricity down there, electricity which I can bear luckily.

"Hamuna kumbozara muno, ndikuda kutowedzera vamwe." the female conductor was saying as the bus took off with the two people it had picked from the second bus stop.

"Driver, don't stop anymore. This bus is so full we can't even move around. Do not love money like this. It's too much now". The kombi and bus drivers don't usually participate in commuter's gruelling activities. The commuters would deal with the conductor so in this case obviously the bus driver didn't respond and kept on driving silently with his head fixed on the road. The drivers also mostly listen to the conductor's demands, if the conductor asks the driver to stop, he stops and if asked to drive he drives. The driver drove for like ten minutes then the bus stopped again. People were now really angry, like fire in the pants angry. A particular short and dark man caught my eye. He was one of the standing passengers and was near the front. I could see in his face that he was pissed and could not stop talking about how unfair this was.

When the bus stopped this time, two people got out. "Better", someone shouted but he had not seen that the bus did not stop only to drop but to pick two people also. Of the two a woman got in first and all the standing passengers went "Aaaaah". The woman was really huge.

The second person was a man but the standing passengers were more concerned about the huge woman. She squeezed herself in and a little space was made for her to fit. She now stood beside the short, dark man. I think their thighs touched because I could see they were standing so close to each other. I could not see down because of the heads in front of me and the other standing passengers. The woman was about the same complexion as the short and dark man but a little taller than him. She was wearing a yellow skirt, a sky blue body top which had seen better days, *yawumbuka*, and a pink and white striped veranda hat. Her one hand was up holding the above pole for support. The bus took off.

According to Newton's third law of motion, as the bus jerked forward at take-off, the woman jerked back and her breast rubbed on the man's arm. I think the man was happy. He had decided to face aside so that his right arm was the one on the woman's side. The man was still complaining but he had toned down his voice a bit and it didn't sound too angry now and when talking he didn't even once look at the woman's face.

"I also want to get home. I am a mother with three children. I have a husband but he is slimmer than me". The woman said in Shona. I tried to connect her also wanting to get home, being a mother and her husband being slimmer than her. I failed to see the connection. Maybe l had missed something they had said to each other in front. I paid more attention.

"Mother madii kutarisa uko", the short man said, signalling the woman to turn and look in front.

"If l turn Mukwasha, it will be much worse. My behind is bigger than my front". Immediately my eyes went straight to her back. I could only see a tip of her back since she was almost facing my direction. The tip of her back was big enough for me to imagine how big her buttocks were and I agreed with her. It certainly will be much worse. Her buttocks were big and round. I looked back at her face. I wanted to see how her face felt about her big buttocks. I saw pride, she was smiling and I could tell it was because of her big buttocks. She surely carried it with confidence and she knew when she walked people would stare and men would be weak to their knees. There was pleasure in her eyes that all these men could see and desire but could not take.

"I have visited the United Kingdom three times", the old man at the seat just behind me said to another man. I didn't turn to check out the other man he was talking to but I imagined they were almost the same age. I had not looked at him when he had walked in when we were still at the Charge Office. I had only heard a greeting exchange between the two of them when they sat side by side. That's when l fully trusted the first old man, I said to myself *Wow, l never imagined people in Zimbabwe could be this nice and polite*. I am used to greetings in kombis in South Africa, the only other country l have visited.

The words United Kingdom are the ones that had caught my attention. Now l was focused on him and had for a bit ceased to listen to the big lady and her short and dark man friend. "And the people from there are very nice and very quiet. They don't shout at each other on buses", he continued. He was referring to the exchanges between the conductor, the big lady and the short dark man since they were the ones with voices being heard louder in the bus. Others were just low grumblings. I imagined he must be retired and all his children are grown and are well off living their lives and inviting *"daddy"* for holidays in the UK. I envied him a little bit though because the UK is on my bucket list and l am a thousand percent sure I will visit it and maybe live there for some time. l don't know. It's funny though when I think about it for a moment, I have a friend from Congo and he says France is on his bucket list, then a friend from Equatorial Guinea, says hers is Spain. I noticed a trend.

We were now near Chigovanyika and the bus stopped and the big lady got off. I looked through the window as she was getting off because I wanted to have a full view of her buttocks and see how it responds to her walking rhythm. From the corner of my right eye I saw that all the standing passengers were as interested as l was and most were male. Some women seated in front of me were too looking out the window at this woman. "Goodbye my daughter." The UK old man interrupted my show.

"Goodbye. *Toonana*". I surprised myself. *Toonana,* why did l say that, it's not like we will see each other again and even if we did, l wouldn't remember his face. I am quite famous when it comes to forgetting people's faces. Anyway l looked back out the window.

The woman walked away and we continued our journey. We arrived at Chigovanyika, the last stop. As l got off l had new confidence. I will walk with that same pride and confidence as the big woman. I will cherish my big butt because it is God's given. I walked with renewed vigour as the late afternoon sun shone on my face, I smiled.

The Approaching Storm
Christopher Kudyahakudadirwe

It was August of '78, eight months after I had completed my O levels. At that time I was naïve, as my friends often described boys like me who had not yet tasted the forbidden fruit. My life had never been influenced or scorched by matters of the heart as well as those of the groin. Then war bombs and machineguns were popcorn all around the countryside but had not yet reached our district. I had passed my O levels with good grades that had given me a place at Tegwani Secondary School to do my A levels, but because Father had run out of the means to raise money for furthering my education, I had to sit out the advancing war and hope for the best afterwards, that is if there was an afterwards.

Then, I was a devout Catholic Youth who, despite the dagga smoking and kachasu drinking that we indulged in in the name of killing time, attended every gathering that was in the cycle of Catholic worship. In this month of August, we went to Chinhoyi for a diocese congress. It was my first time to be in Chinhoyi, so besides being a big Catholic meeting, for me it was a tour that expanded my spatial horizon of Zimbabwe-Rhodesia. Our parish hired a bus to take us there and that too was an experience worth archiving in my eighteen-year-old memory. I had never been outside my district since I started Sub A. The only fading memory I had was when Mother took us to Gatooma on a train when Father had been arrested for political reasons in '64.

I had money. Since January of that year, I had been working at the mission earning a dollar per day. That was a lot of money for a teenager like me. Although there were many church members going, a distant brother of my mother, who was three or four years older than me, was the only person related to me in the entire entourage.

We had become great buddies since we worked together as general hands at the mission.

We drank, smoked and sought after the company of girls although I was still an amateur. He often told me in minute details about what he had done with some of the girls who were with us on the bus. Uncle was like my mentor when it came to these worldly indulgencies that boys of our age sought after.

The activities of the three-day congress were timetabled in such a way that during the day we attended conferences and religious teachings from the very many brothers and nuns as well as catechists from all corners of the diocese. Lunch was served from one o'clock to about half past three and then we went back for music lessons. It was during this lunch time that Uncle tracked down two girls from the other side of our parish whom I had never met before but were known to him very well.

"I know them from the time we were building their church in Bvochora," Uncle said as he introduced them to me. Uncle had been in the employment of the mission longer than me; hence he knew people from outreach church sites I had not visited.

One of the girls was one of Uncle's girlfriends. Uncle always boasted that he had a girlfriend at each of the outreach churches that the priest we worked with and went to say mass on Sunday.

"This here is Letwin. Letwin, this is my nephew, Chake." We shook hands.

Uncle pulled his girlfriend away from us so that they could have their space and time away from us two strangers.

Letwin was a shy petite girl whom I fell in love with as soon as I saw her. She had a dimple in her left cheek which only showed when she smiled. This made me feel I had a daunting task of making her smile so that I can always be rewarded with that beautiful dimple all the time. Her dark complexion, complemented by the smoothness of her skin and the whiteness of her teeth, appealed to me so much that before she had admitted to loving me back, I had already started treating her like my girlfriend, and she did not object to this.

Supper was served as from half past five up until eight. That evening we were at the head of the queue for food so that we can have ample time to be with our girlfriends before evening programmes started later at quarter-past eight. After we had eaten and cleaned our plates and packed them away, we took a walk into the township of Chikonohono with our girlfriends. We bought them drinks and garlic polony and sat on the front of the shops as we chatted them up. Later, we took them to the periphery of the church yard, and there we kissed and fondled just like all young lovers do. It was my first time to do such amorous things with and to any girl. Before that, I had had to steal snatches of girls' breasts and then suffer the consequences of being scolded like a rabid dog. Letwin became my goddess who could provide such niceties of life without beating me off shamefully.

So, after the three-day congress had wound up and we had suspended our relationships with our girlfriends since we were going our separate ways, exchanged love tokens such as handkerchiefs and necklaces, the hired bus took us back where we belonged. We looked into each other's eyes as if we were not going to see each other again.

*

Before one is inducted into the Catholic Church to partake in the body of the son of man and sometimes drink his blood from the golden goblet, one must be baptised in the name of the Father, the Son and the Holy Spirit. Only then could one say that they belong to this church, participate in the ceremonies and masses that are part of it. Initially Letwin did not like to be a Catholic. It was her friend who had dragged her to come along. The journey to Chinhoyi had been her first experience of Catholicism.

Those who wanted to be baptised came to the mission at the beginning of December for the catechism. From the four corners of the parish, the young and old people came with their bags full of their clothes and blankets and pots and plates. We, being local, welcomed them with the expectations of lovers who had been missing their lovers for over four months. Every evening, therefore, we went to the mission hall to practise singing with them and after that we would take our girls to dark corners of the mission yard and talk to them and do the little things we could do to each other. My standing ovation would raise the whole auditorium and light up the lights in my head making them flicker on and off, signalling the presence of exciting danger. It was during these few times that I had really come into close bodily contact with a girl therefore whatever little things we did to each other were treasured and consigned to the back of my memory for future reference and narration to my peers. This created a bubble of happiness in which I existed as a man and no longer as a boy. I could now stand in front of other boys and narrate my experiences with women with conviction. During those days, like a hallo above the head of an angel, the bubble of triumph was always with me wherever I went.

When things are happening smoothly, and everything beautiful seems to come one's way, it is wise to expect a jolting bump that will wake one to the realities of life. For me, this moment arrived one Saturday afternoon. My Saturdays always started by going to the fields to weed in between the sprouting maize or cotton plants. Around eleven, we would put our hoes on our shoulders and go home for breakfast. Afterwards we would take our towels and go to the river to bath. So, on this Saturday, the same routine ran its course and by one o'clock I was on my way to the mission to see Letwin.

When I arrived at the mission buildings, the hot December sun was leaning slightly to the west. Drops of perspiration were rolling down my forehead like raindrops on the windscreen of a car without wipers. Huge towering thunderstorm clouds were gathering in the north and the slight breeze rushing from that direction was bringing the smell of wet earth to my nose. Sparks of metallic lightening were jumping across the peaks of the clouds to be punctuated by delayed rumblings of thunder.

Since it was just after lunch, most of the catechumens were lounging on the verandas of the mission buildings. Some were reciting the Lord's Prayer while others were cramming the Ten Commandments the way Moses could have done when he received them from God. A few others were singing hymns they had learnt recently. However, my eyes were looking for her only.

She was not among those who were reciting the Lord's Prayer nor those cramming the Ten Commandments like Moses. I expected to find her among the few who were singing the hymns they had recently been taught, but she was not there. She was not even among those who were practising rosary prayers. Where could she be?

In the north the thunderstorm was approaching, seemingly unbothered by the fact that I had failed to locate Letwin among all the catechumens on the mission. The flashing lightning and the rumbling thunder were now coming closer to happening at the same time. The lightning would flash, and I would breathe in and out about five times before the accompanying thunderclaps became the full stop to the dialogue between the two. The heat was like that from an oven, and the air was thick one would mould a morsel of it. Above us, a pair of bateleur eagles rode on the shoulders of the boiling air.

When I asked the other catechumens where Letwin was, they all looked at me with eyes that had a message, but I did not understand it. Some looked away or down when I continued to enquire about my girlfriend. They all knew she was the one I came to see there, even the catechists who were teaching them catechism knew that because whenever I came to the mission, I asked for her.

The storm that was brewing in the north was now almost upon us. The strong smell of wet earth was thick in the air. The mutowa trees that stood around the buildings were now swaying like drunk giants caught in a whirlwind in the dry season. The wind whistled through their long thin branches nipping off those that were not

117

strongly attached to the trunks. People who had been walking around sought shelter on the verandas of the mission buildings. I also joined them as we watched the approaching storm tear across the open fields towards the south. Soon large drops of rain started bombing the dusty ground here and there, sending miniature dust clouds into the air, drumming the corrugated iron roofs above our heads like that Rare Earth rock band drummer getting mad at the end of their 21-minute-long song, 'Get Ready'. Without warning there was a giant spark which was immediately followed by an ear-splitting crack of thunder. We all fell to the floor in knee-jerk reactions to the thunder.

When I stood up from where I had fallen, the door to one of the rooms cracked open. Out stumbled Andrew one of the catechists, dazed. His zip was undone. I looked at his face. Beads of sweat were all over and some were dripping down soaking his shirt. Behind him, I espied my girlfriend, Letwin. She too was dazed. Her dress was almost up to her waist. At first the two did not recognise me. The crack of thunder had dazed them as much as it had dazed all of us who were taking shelter under the veranda. She was also sweating as much as Andrew was. I was confused. My heart started beating the drum in my chest. My ears were burning as if they were on fire. There was a storm of confused emotions inside me. Strong surges of anger and bewilderment were blowing inside me. Why were these two coming from the same room and in that dishevelled state? The Lucifer in me was urging me to pick up someone and throw them into the inferno of my rage. But then the Gabriel in me was advising me to be cautious and not do things I would regret later.

By now the heavens had broken loose and a deluge was coming down as gusts of strong wind blew into my face. All my youthful life I was a person who was terrified by thunderstorms but on this day, without giving it a thought, I headed into the approaching storm for I knew that the storm inside my chest needed calming. Maybe the cool raindrops could be the solution.

A Little Song for The Young One
Matthew K Chikono

She didn't have to look at her wristwatch to know she was going to be late to work, again. The previous week her new employer had let it slide but she knew this time they wouldn't. She tried to quicken her pace, it didn't help much, she was old and slow. Fifty-three years old, that wasn't young at all.

Quarter to six. It was almost dark, and the streets were getting empty. It was good, darkness got rid of smelly unwashed bodies from the streets of Durban. She preferred to walk in the evening breeze on her way to work, in peace and silence whilst enveloped in her own dark thoughts.

"Salibonani Mama Zodwa!" A man from a banana stall greeted her as she passed. She raised her hand and waved at him, she didnt have enough time to return a proper greeting and to chat. Besides if she were to greet everyone she knew, she wouldn't ever arrive to her destination. She knew everyone in the city, well, almost everyone in the city. She had been born there. At thirteen Mama Zodwa had started working as a maid, nanny and a laundry lady. Heck, she even delivered fresh milk to hundreds of people who lived in the eastern side of Durban. It wasn't a wonder why everyone knew her, and a lot of people offered her jobs. She only accepted those job offers if children happened to be involved.

Despite the September evening being warm Mama Zodwa donned a long brown and black dress, a wrapping towel was thrown over her shoulders and her grey hair was uncovered, short and well-trimmed. On her feet she wore knee-length black socks and high heels shoes which made a clacking sound on the paved driveway as she arrived at her workplace.

She found Ms. Pete impatiently tapping the door handle, waiting for her arrival. Ms. Pete was young, twenty-five maybe, and was from Greece. It might not be the reason why her kind of dressing was weird; a strapless tiny blouse, mini-skirt, and high heels all in black. It was this kind of revealing clothes she left wearing those Thursday evening when she hired Mama Zodwa to stay over for the night with her seven-year-old son, Jeremy.

"You are late," Ms. Pete said grabbing her handbag and keys, "next time I want to be so forgiving."

She didn't wait for Mama Zodwa to reply before dashing out to the driveway where her car was parked. Mama Zodwa's greeting was left on her lips.

"She's definitely a prostitute," Mama Zodwa said to no one as she made her way to Jeremy's bedroom, "or else how would she afford this luxurious house."

Jeremy was reading his favourite storybook, about cows, giants, and a boy, whilst he lay on his tiny bed. He looked up as Mama Zodwa bulged in the boy's room without knocking. A minute smile tried to form on his lip, but it died without reaching his grey eyes. He was already in his pajamas. Jeremy was a chubby and an unhappy boy.

Mama Zodwa took out a lunchbox of mashed potatoes and gave it to the boy in silence. Ms. Pete had forgotten to prepare something for his son to eat before she went on those nights, more often than expected of a young single mother. Mama Zodwa wasn't sure if that day was one of them, it was confirmed seconds later when the boy garnished the contents of the lunchbox with his bare hands. Half a minute later he was laying on the bed staring on the ceiling with a satisfied look on his face.

"Will you tell me the story of the fisherman again before I sleep Mama Zodwa?"

"No dear one, tonight I will sing for you one of my favorites folklore song my grandmother taught me but first let me go and lock up and do the dishes." She replied with her smothering motherly voice.

The boy gave a small smile as Mama Zodwa left the room for the kitchen, she found it in disarray. Pots and pans on the floor. Plates and spoons, from last week's lunch with the priest, were stashed in the sink and under the table. Mama Zodwa cursed before she started washing them.

She thought to herself how it would be nice to have such money and a beautiful home like Ms. Pete's. She didn't know what Ms. Pete did for a living but what she knew was; that every Thursday evening Mama Zodwa was called upon to babysit Jeremy for the whole night. Ms. Pete would leave wearing fancy clothes only to return the next morning still looking fresh and young. Without saying any word Ms. Pete would hand her a couple of 200 Rand notes, Mama Zodwa would accept them and take her leave without questions. It still would be nice if she could afford those fancy things and food like her employer. Surely with all this money Mama Zodwa would finally be able to afford a doctor who would treat her aliment properly.

She was old, sick, and dying.

A strange curse was coursing through her veins, causing her pain and temporary paralysis. Since birth, Mama Zodwa had suffered from such disease that no witchdoctor had been able to cure her. She did found relief in children though, a little lick or suck of the young one's blood restored her healthy, just for a couple of days though, but it was not enough to call a life.

After washing the dishes, Mama Zodwa cleaned the kitchen and went back to Jeremy's room. He was still awake, waiting for his favourite nanny. Mama tucked him in and lay beside him on the tiny bed. Jeremy didn't have to beg twice before Mama Zodwa started to sing to him. It might have been a hymn, it might have been a chant, the difference between the lyrics and the incarnations were lost to the little boy who drowsed to the feminine voice which sliced the night with its Zulu enchantments. It was no ordinary folklore, Mama Zodwa knew of its magic.

Few minutes later it had done its job; Jeremy, who was now half asleep, grabbed Mama Zodwa's hand and begged her not to leave his side. From the trance he murmured something about a kiss on the forehead and how it would help him sleep better. Mama hesitated for a second, a tingle of guilty ripped from her heart before she savagely kissed him until a drop of blood fell. She licked it and decided to take the opportunity to live a little longer. She put her mouth back on the tiny wound, sucked a little more blood. She couldn't resist. She sucked some more; she did not let go until the sunrise.

BOTEREKWA
Dumisani Charles Kufaruwenga

A lovely road descended from the mountains of the small mining town of Shurugwi in a south-easterly direction, towards another small mining town of Zvishavane.

It is said the road was constructed by the Italians around 1945 during the Second World War, who used mostly the labour of prisoners of war to accomplish the task.

It was an engineering feat of majestic proportions. At some of its portions, the road hangs precariously like a shelf in the side of the mountain cliff, and in other parts it snakes smoothly on the summit of the mountain, oblivious of its own perilous, terrifying height. The road then descends sharply down a steep slope towards Zvishavane, and gracefully straightens out.

It had breathtaking views on either side with evergreen plush vegetation resembling the equatorial rain forest.

The white man named it Wolfshall Pass, but the locals call it "Boterekwa", which means the winding way.

The road still exists, but with none of its grandeur.

It is now riddled with pot-holes and the vegetation on its sides is being hacked away by artisanal gold miners. These miners dig everywhere for gold, leaving large, ugly, gaping and dangerous holes. They even dig tunnels underneath the surface, crossing the road. At one stage the road at the steep slopes of the Zvishavane end of Boterekwa collapsed because of these underground tunnels.

The artisanal miners are generally rowdy and lawless and violent. They steal and fight and die when dangerous tunnels and unsafe mine shafts collapse. They damage the environment and choke the rivers with the mountains of the soil they dig up, which is swept downriver by the rain. And for the saddest part, they destroy the spectacular beauty of Boterekwa, the winding way.

It is because of this behaviour of the artisanal miners from which the acronym "MaShurugwi" was derived.

"MaShurugwi" is a word which is used to describe violent machete wielding gangs who take over rich gold mining locations using force.

But few have made a difference in their lives by exploiting gold. Most still live in poverty and go back to their dilapidated homes in the village, with absolutely nothing. Only a handful have bought a few herd of cattle, and one or two have bought stands in urban areas where they are constructing modest houses.

This notwithstanding, hordes of unemployed youths still flock to Boterekwa in search of gold, leaving it scarred and ugly and collapsing, leaving the village without the much needed labour for agricultural activities.

It is therefore almost impossible to find someone to employ in the village to tend cattle and till the land, everyone is possessed with the madness of the gold rush.

Everyone.

And a family working in Harare has a rural home in Shurugwi, some fifty or so kilometers from Boterekwa.

After struggling to find someone to look after their ancestral home, the family who works in Harare was referred to a young couple with one child who were willing to stay at their home, tilling the land and tending the cattle, in exchange of a modest wage and adequate food rations.

The young couple consisted of two different characters. The husband was talkative and full of l know. The wife was withdrawn.

So the urban family entrusted "Talkative" and "Reticent" with their ancestral home and retreated to Harare.

After some time, word was sent to the Harare urban family that Talkative had been arrested for theft, and that Reticent was now alone at their ancestral home.

Details of how and why Talkative had been arrested were sketchy, but the general thrust was that Talkative was part of a gang which waylaid haulage trucks as they ascended or descended Boterekwa. As the haulage trucks slowly negotiated the steep slopes of Boterekwa, Talkative's gang would leap onto the load from a vantage point, cut up the truck's tent with knives, offload goods from the truck and flee.

Two members of the urban family drove from Harare and raced down to Shurugwi to find out what had happened.

Reticent knew very little about the arrest. She told them that Talkative had told her that he had been asked by a relative who owed him money to accompany the relative to Shurugwi to collect his money. According to Talkative's account to Reticent, the relative and another gang member were on a mission to steal, a fact Talkative didn't know at the time he agreed to accompany them to Shurugwi. When they reached Boterekwa, so the story went, the other two disappeared into the night towards the road, leaving Talkative at a secluded place. The two returned with what they called "their" goods, and Talkative helped them carry the goods into Shurugwi town.

Whilst they were in Shurugwi, the police pounced, and the other two fled, leaving Talkative alone with what turned out to be goods which had been stolen from a vehicle which was driving up the steep slopes of Boterekwa.

Talkative insisted that he was innocent, and had asked Reticent to plead with the family for help.

Before committing themselves, the two family members decided to find out the truth. They questioned Reticent closely.

"This relative who came to take Talkative, where is he?

125

Reticent replied;

"He is working at a relative's place in the village to the east, where he is hiding from the police."

So the two family members drove to the local rural police station and presented their story to the Officer-In-Charge.

The Officer-In-Charge wasn't interested in raiding a suspect. He had more important things to do. A senior politician was visiting Shurugwi town and his officers had to be deployed to meet the senior politician. Besides, he had no vehicle, and strictly speaking, this wasn't his case, it belonged to Shurugwi where the theft occurred. "Sorry, can't help you gentlemen", he dismissed them.

The two family members could not back down. They offered their car for the raid, they pleaded with the Officer-In-Charge, they offered to purchase refreshments for the raiding party, and to meet all expenses associated with the raid. Suddenly, the Officer-In-Charge had manpower, and asks if the two family members would be happy to be escorted by two officers?

And off to the village to the east they went, the two police officers and the two family members. They discussed strategy along the way.

Members of the village to the east were co-operative. They explained that "Suspect" had taken the cattle to the pastures. They agreed to send one of them to bring Suspect and the cattle home, under the guise that someone wanted to buy a cow from the herd wanted to see it first. It was also agreed that the two family members would pose as buyers, whilst the two uniformed police officers would hide in the house, where the unsuspecting Suspect would be led. Members of the village also agreed to pretend to be going about their business normally while they were actually on the look out for any attempt by Suspect to escape.

The stage was set.

As pre-arranged, the unsuspecting Suspect and another villager brought the cattle. As they approached the home where Suspect worked, Suspect spotted the car belonging to the two family members, and immediately became suspicious. He spun around and faced the other villager who accompanied him;

"Whose car is that?"

The villager who accompanied Suspect replied as calmly as possible:

"It belongs to the buyers who have come to purchase the cow."

But Suspect's antenna was up.

"It means they've brought the police. Buyers always bring the police to clear the cattle they want to buy. I'm out of here."

With that, Suspect bolted to the east and sped off.

The villagers were ready for Suspect. They ran and intercepted him and caught him and brought him before the two police officers, and one of the police officers rose dramatically and whipped out his handcuffs and slapped them around Suspect's wrists. He smiled proudly at everyone present and said;

"I'm the one who has has arrested him."

The two family members, the two police officers with Suspect between them, drove back to the local rural police station.

Along the way, Suspect sang like a bird;

"Although it was his first time, Talkative knew our mission right from the start. The big boss promised us money if we helped him pull off the job. No, we didn't steal from a lorry. Yes, we stole from the luggage compartment of a bus which was coming from South Africa. Big Boss is the one who opened the luggage compartment while the bus was in motion. Big Boss threw the stolen goods our way, and Talkative and myself whisked the goods away."

When the raiding party arrived at the local rural police station, the Officer-In-Charge, instead of rejoicing, began castigating the raiding crew.

"What must I now do with the prisoner you've brought? You make my job difficult. I've no transport to take him to Shurugwi, I've no phone to alert Shurugwi that I have their prisoner, what do you want me to do?

The two family members would have none of it. They told the Officer-In-Charge to make a plan, and drove off after leaving Suspect. The Officer-In-Charge ran after their car, yelling for help, until the car disappeared from view.

Talkative and Suspect were both convicted of an offence, which in legal parlance, is called "Theft From Car" and were both sentenced to nine (9) months imprisonment with labour.

The family relieved Reticent of her duties and sent her away. Their ancestral home is now without a gate keeper, the gate keepers having been swallowed by the allure of Boterekwa, the winding way, the place of death, deception, desolation and destruction.

The place that was once scenic and serene.

Where did all the birds go?
Matthew Kunashe Chikono

After the news-paper had packed their cameras and left, Lukia walked over to the river bank where her aunt had been left standing alone. She was gazing into the water as if someone was about to come out of it. Lukia relied her father's message to her. Lukia had known the message wouldn't be well received, she was just a messenger hoping not to get shot. Her aunt stood for a moment staring into Lukia's eyes, her face twitching as evil thoughts ran wild in her mind.

"Your mother, she is the one who send you, isn't she?" Aunty Firidha said heaving in anger, "My brother would never say such things to me, that wife of his is always imposing her will. Go and tell her that if she doesn't like the way I am handling the situation she should come and tell me herself."

Lukia lowered her head, utterly disgusted by her aunt, and started walking back home. It was a kilometer or so from the river to the homestead where she lived with her family. It wasn't the distance that made her heart unsettle - she was accustomed to the distance - but the thought of vanishing whilst walking past the woodlot between the river and her family's homestead. Disappearing without leaving a trace, just like her sister.

Handling the situation, that was what her aunt had called it. The way she had been handling the situation was to dress like a teenage and talk about how her niece had been taken by the mermaid that lived in the River Save whenever the camera people arrived. Aunt Firidha had become the self-appointed family spokesperson, Lukia's father had sent her to tell her aunt to stop doing that after she had left with another group of camera people who had arrived that morning. Her aunt had went berserk on her, accusing Lukia's mother of being a horrible sister-in-law.

The woodlot Lukia had to pass on her way from the river consisted of pine and gum trees. If someone was to abduct her, they would have an excellent place to set an ambush for her. Lukia listened carefully as she walked through the whistling pine trees that Friday afternoon. If an attacker was to show themselves, Lukia wasn't going to scream for help. No, she couldn't, she had to fight for herself. At sixteen, Lukia was as healthy as any child of her age. Village life had toughened her since birth.

The woodlot was quiet, too quiet to make Lukia feel relaxed though. Not a sound of a chirping cricket could be heard. Lukia also realised there weren't any birds singing in the trees too. For a moment she wondered where all the birds had gone. She thought maybe they had day jobs in the fields where they caught worms and ate maize cobs and would return to their nests in the evening. Lukia missed the birds. When she was younger she had been taught by someone that the absence of singing birds was a permutation of something bad going to happen-like getting kidnapped in the woodlot.

Often lately, Lukia had been getting thoughts of being abducted whenever she was alone. She had also started having nightmares about men putting a black bag on her head and taking her with them and she unable to scream for help. She couldn't scream if anything like that were to happen to her. Not a single word had passed from her mouth since birth. The invading thoughts of being kidnapped had started after her sister's disappearance, about a fortnight earlier. Lukia wanted to believe her sister had been kidnapped and would be returned to them as soon as her father paid a certain number of heifers. Her father had dozens of those and surely could afford to exchange some, if not all, for the safe return of her eldest daughter. The kidnapping story was more feasible in Lukia's mind than the story her family was dishing out to the public; their daughter had been taken by the mermaid of Save River and would be returned to them if they perform the necessary ceremony and ritual at the riverbank.

It was way past lunch when Lukia finally arrived home. The three mud huts and a bricked cottage was the only home she had ever known. A strange car was parked outside. Obviously, she didn't know whom it belonged to, none of their relatives or fellow villagers owned cars. Lukia prayed it wasn't the news people again trying to write a story about her missing sister. Over the past few days she had grown to hate everyone who asked about Eustancia.

Lukia crunched and silently moved closer to one of the hut the family used as a kitchen. That was where her mother would receive visitors. The smell of cooking chicken made her mouth to water. They only cooked chicken for important guest, not journalists or camera people. A sigh of relief left her mouth, she was certain that she had been saved a trip to the river.

She wasn't going to bulge in the house without knowing how important the visitor was, she didn't want to embarrass her family or herself. First, she listened through the wall and could hear a muffled voice. It was her mother's, recounting for the thousandth time the night of Eustancia's disappearance.

"Then I told her to go to the river to fetch a bucket of water for the chickens, you know the rains haven't fallen well this month. It was almost seven in the evening when I realised she wasn't back yet," Lukia's mother's voice broke a bit, "knowing my daughter well, my maternal instinct told me that something was wrong. I sent her father and her uncle to look for her."

At that moment the story was interrupted whilst her mother sobbed. Lukia could hear her uncle, Aunt Firidha's young brother, telling her not to cry for it was a bad omen to mourn for someone who was not yet dead. Despite her uncle being the youngest in her father's family, he sounded wise most of the time that Lukia was both surprised and impressed at the same time.

After few minutes or so, her mother regained her composure and continued the story," They followed her all by the way to the river. They couldn't find her, but what they did find on the riverside was her

131

bucket, her sandals, and her wrapping cloth neatly folded on top of the bucket."

With the tale complete, Lukia made her way into the hut to see whom the story was being narrated to. She entered the room to find her uncle sitting on the only bench in the house with rich-looking man. He was dark and had a well-rounded belly. On the other side of the room, her mother sat on the mat with the fairest of the woman of the country. The woman looked familiar but Lukia couldn't figure out where she had seen her before.

Lukia shook hands with each of the strangers and went to hid herself behind her mother. Lukia's mother apologised for her behavior and told the strangers about her daughter's condition.

"Lukia doesn't speak but she could hear and knows sign language. She is Eustancia's younger sister, three years apart." her mother continued," You see pastor, our whole family is not doing well and we need your help."

Pastor. The man was the pastor at a church Eustancia attended. The woman was his wife, now Lukia remembered where she had seen the woman before. Few days before her disappearance, Eustancia had dragged Lukia to church. It was strange since Eustancia was the only one in the whole family who went to church. It made sense for Eustancia to go to church; she was nineteen and looking for a husband. After the service, Eustancia had pointed to the pastor's wife and whispered into Lukia's ear," She is your father's girlfriend. I saw them kissing last week behind the grocery store."

Lukia didn't know how to react when she had heard the gossip. Now with the woman sitting comfortable beside her mother she didn't know what it meant. She wondered again how the holiest of the woman in the village had managed to meet her father who didn't go to church and spent his time at beer halls with loud noises. No answer came here. Lukia kept her eyes on the door waiting for her father to bust in and do something.

Nothing happened. Her father come back home early evening, hours after the pastor and his wife had left. He didn't come alone, he was in company of two men. They didn't go inside the house, but straight to the cattle kraal where they stood and pointed at different heifers at irregular intervals. After an hour or so the two men left. Her father went to the kitchen where Lukia was preparing supper in the presence of her mother.

"The village headman and the witch doctor just left." He proclaimed. No one said anything, not even his two younger siblings.

"The doctor said we should pay him one beast and another cow shall be slaughtered for the ceremony," her father continued, "the headman had agreed that the ceremony be done two nights from now."

"You can't do the ceremony that night," Lukia's mother's finally spoke, "Eustancia's pastor will be doing an all-night church service at the river bank to bring back my daughter."

Her father stood up, upsetting the bench. He puffed with anger, "You think you are now the man of the house who does all the thinking? Did you think this through? What if you are upsetting the mermaid by doing the Jesus stuff at the river? Do you think my daughter will be safe?"

Aunt Firidha intervened and tried to sooth her brother's anger by kneeling on the floor and begging for the soft side of the Hog totem. Her older brother didn't have time for that, he even lashed at her, "Don't pretend you even care Firidha! You are enjoying the attention the news people are giving you. You think you are going to be a celebrity because you will be on TV and YouTube? You need to get another husband and leave my house. Or go and beg the first one to take you back."

Lukia continued cooking on the fire place, she didn't have the voice to give her opinion. She could see her uncle sitting quietly in the dim hut, listening and waiting for the perfect moment to chip in. In the end it didn't matter; her father was the first to storm out of the hut, probably to a beer hall, her aunt unable to look at her sister-in-law escaped to her sleeping quarters, and her mother with red eyes, from the loss of the battle of words, excused herself and went to cry in her bedroom.

Lukia continued cooking and she knew that night only her uncle and her would be having supper. The trio wouldn't be back until the following morning. The scene that had played in front of Lukia wasn't a new one. Fighting had been happening almost every day since Eustancia had vanished. They were the same and always solved nothing.

"Everyone is on edge these days," her uncle finally Said, "they should calm down and solve this like a real family."

Lukia dished the dried okra she had cooked as the relish for the night. She handed it along with a plate of sadza and a dish of water for him to wash his hands. Her uncle starting eating near the fireplace where the light was better. Lukia took that opportunity to closely look at the man her sister had called 'the devil of the family'.

He was around twenty eight, dark and short. He was the sweetest member of the family, after Eustancia of course. Lukia couldn't imagine what the horrible thing he had done to Eustancia many times that she would consider telling the police and calling him a devil.

"It's considered rude to stare at people like that while they are eating." Her uncle said eventually noticing her.

Lukia hand mentioned what she thought she would never tell anyone.

"Maybe Eustancia left to find her real father because everyone in this family is horrible to her, especially you. You deserve to go to jail for taking advantage of her."

"That was a lot of words and I didn't understand any of it, well, except for father and Eustancia. What I think is she has eloped with that boyfriend of hers who works in Harare. She should have appreciated how much your mother and father loves you." Her uncle said.

Our father, the words echoed in Lukia's ears. My father, Lukia thought, he is not Eustancia's father. She wanted to scream until her father heard that the daughter he had raised for 19 years wasn't his. Lukia knew it, Eustancia knew it and her mother knew it but her father and his siblings didn't.

For two whole days none of the family members spoke to Lukia, except for her uncle. To be fair no one in the family spoke to anyone. With the day of ceremony to appease the mermaid of the river, the family hated each other more. Lukia's mother had decided not to heed to her husband, and was determined to let the pastor host his church service at the river the same night as the ceremony.

On the morning of that day, Lukia's uncle joked that it was better to ask both the spirit of the river and the Holy Spirit for the safe return of Eustancia. The joke was received with stony and awkward silence. He shrugged and went on with his life, which on that day included slaughtering a cow to be consumed at the riverbank during the ceremony.

Lukia helped cook and carry pots of food and beer. There was lots of it, traditional millet beer, pots and jars filled to the brim. It was an essential component of the ceremony. Lukia knew only a cup would be used for the ceremony, the rest was to lure villagers to grace the event. Who wouldn't want free beer?

Apparently the pastor, his promiscuous wife, and their congregation didn't want the free beer. The presence of the ancient liquid was so repulsive to the pastor's wife that she started crying. Lukia desperately wanted to ask her if fermented millet was worse than adultery among the Ten Commandments. Lukia searched the overcrowded River bank for her father. She wanted to see if he was also watching the drama his extra marital partner was acting. She found him standing a distance away, his back turned from the church people. He doesn't want people to notice the chemistry between him and the pastor's wife, Lukia thought, or Eustancia lied there is nothing at all between them.

She kept one eye on the pastor's wife and another on her father. The moment a tear dropped from the wife's eye, a dozen handkerchiefs were offered to her. Being a woman of God she only accepted her husband's only. Her fellow women from church spread cloth on the ground for her to sit whilst she recovered. Lukia smiled, it was funny. How can a woman like that do it with her father? She prayed that her father would come over to her and explain his side of the story.

Her prayer was answered. Suddenly his father turned and started walking towards her. People who had turned up for the ceremony eyed him sympathetically whilst they made way for him to pass. However a hint of anger was on his face. Lukia knew he was coming to vent off. Everyone vented off to her. They came to complain about others to her. They told her their secrets. She was a mute and wasn't supposed to say a single word about. Lukia listened without complaining.

"Look at your aunt over there." His father hissed when he was in earshot, "Dressed like a common whore for the cameras."

Aunty Firidha was dressed in a tiny dress that left her ugly legs bare. A thick layer of makeup was on her face. She looked pretty. Aunty Firidha was directing and giving instructions to the small newspaper interns who had came to cover the event. She was enjoying herself.

"I don't think she cares for my daughter at all." His father said with a resigned look on his face.

Lukia stared at his face and let her hands drop. She didn't have it in her to tell his father Eustancia wasn't his biological daughter. As if he had read her mind his father said, "Eustancia is my daughter, I raised her for 19 years."

Their father-daughter moment was interrupted by screams. A fight had started. From afar Lukia could see the pastor punching his wife. No, not his wife. He was punching the witch doctor who had slapped his wife. The church people were now trying to form a wall to protect their holy one. The horde of beer people stumbled and staggered to help the village headman who had been trapped in the middle trying to broker peace between the two camps.

Lukia could see no one caring about her sister.

Lukia's noticed her mother on the ground. Her father noticed his wife in need of comfort and protection and dashed over to console her, or scold her. Lukia wasn't sure what would happen. Her uncle stood a distance away, tearing with his mouth the meat from the cow he had slaughtered. Aunty Firidha stood alone with her hands on her waist, her army of newspaper interns scrambling away to take pictures of the great twist to the boring ceremony.

Lukia started walking away, upstream were she knew there were no hippos or crocodiles. She could hear the sound of the uproar turning in a whisper behind her. She looked at the slow moving water and begged it to bring her sister back. There was no answer. She asked the river if her sister had left all the madness, left her and her horrible family to a better life. She strained her ears not to miss a whisper from the river. There was silence, not even the birds chirped to console her on that September sunset. Lukia wondered again, where all the birds had gone.

To escape or to overwhelm

Tendai Rinos Mwanaka

To escape or to overwhelm are two love's dangerous animals... I always uncannily choose not to cling to the shirtsleeves of a current. Aren't we most dangerous when we are in love? Imagine the people we have send to early graves because of our love, the ocean of tears we created, the anguish, the brokenness that's an ever-present fever, the fulcrum of passion whittling away at what was once us. They are a few instances I allowed love to overwhelm me, and I still nurse the wounds... frayed, scared, now closed, the only product are the memories. For none of my loves have grown to create offsprings that I can look back on. It always dies a Gavamwedzi. In Shona language a still birth is known as Gavamwedzi, "half-moon". And we can't throw our arms around the half moon, warming upon the half-moon's heat. It was already cold before it showed up.

And I think all the memories that are worth writing about happen when you are young, for afterwards you start subtracting yourself.

I was at the edge of seventeen and totally in love, my first voyage into the treacle world of relationships. It's her mother I am writing about now.

Something greyish in the crows' voice, their crazy fingerling angry haunting cries at me, as if I had stood in their paths and blocked their sun in the open skies above my fields, makes me think about her, the mother. And the soft mourning of a hoe as I weed my veggies' beds, low in the dark black soils of South East Harare has a quiet unlacing feeling. And the few wafts of white cotton clouds grace the western rim of the valley; I could hear the soft drones of vehicles passing through Seke Road on their way to Harare or to Chitungwiza. It's a late autumn afternoon, the rains are fizzling out here and there. Summer is gone. These crows have been flying all over my paths to the fields too, as if they had a message they were trying to relay on to me, and they were irritated with myself for ignoring them.

And yet, her image as she turned dark with anger but held herself back from exploding, seeing me with her daughter in a cozy intimate position beside the road to home never dies in my memories. We were on our way home, Friday afternoon's half-school day's feelings and the overblown teenage hormones cursing through us as we steamed ourselves, off each other's' succulent bodies. Frenching it, I had her top shirt off, licking her two girls, the centre of my universe and then she was upon us like an evil spirit.

"Murikuitei vana imi", in a crowed voice full of anger she rattled me out of her cleavage. You don't wait to answer and tell her you were milking her. It felt like I was milking the mother. I took to my feet, bursting off into the fields instead of the way to home which was just hundreds of metres away. Going home was out of question as she could have followed me home and shamed me in front of my mother. *Let her tell her later,* I thought as my feet got me beyond her fangled up anger. She shouted at her daughter and told her to go home, and that she will deal with her later. It was obvious she would deal with her with sticks and stones.

She was on her way to the shops so she hurtled off to the South as we trundled off to the North. I catch up with my lover a hundred or so metres and tried to comfort her. She was quiet, troubled and I knew that was the end of it. The mother would make sure of it.

But the mother couldn't succeed in breaking Kresenzia and me apart though; it's me who later broke us apart. I chose my favourite: to escape.

The crows continued their abuse of the surroundings with their throat corroded caterwauls as I thought of how much she had disguised her detest of me as I ran through girls who looked like her daughters, like toilet paper. I was a shit teen, always seeking fleeting attention and backing off when it was too hot, always shitting on everything good I come across. In actual fact back then I just broke things; cups, plates, glasses, pens, books… it was one thing I knew I could do and that I was unbelievably good at, whether I consciously wanted to do it or not. I thought even my gaze could break things up.

I broke her grandma's heart when she saw me 3 months later in an intimate position with Kresenzia's sister, Karen; thereby ending that relationship. I think she was watching us from afar, because the way she just happen to pass besides the ditch we were sheltering in where there was no road to anywhere, in the middle of the forests, was curious. I think she thought we were learning our first alphabet. Lucky, we were just messing around, clothes on. I am sure I was going to get a wife if it was otherwise. And I decided to break my heart for a couple of years more trying to win Karen back. She trying to hurt me as much as possible to avenge for the hurt I had caused her and Kresenzia. And for years I was caught up in the cycle of leaving and returning to Kresenzia and Karen. I loved both, the one who broke me and the one who made me whole. From that day onwards I knew how it hurts to lose someone you loved without knowing you do. And as I got older I have realized how the sisters must have felt, why the mum detested me and the grandmother could barely answer my greetings ever afterwards, webbing us in unease silence for a lifetime. Love has come to mean escape for me. To escape all this subtraction I try to keep to myself, to avoid falling in love, to stench off this corrosion that is a constant ache upon me.

"I saw your father at the funeral of my departed Auntie and your father was joking with my friend. My friend had told your father that I am his muroora."

"Kkkkkk," I laughed before I asked her,

"Who is this Auntie who died", and added, "how can you claim to be my wife when you haven't seen me for a year, haven't spoken to me for some time."

"It's Maiguru Mai Kresenzia who passed away", and I am like,

"You are not serious, she died…, when. Why. I can't believe this."

Of course I had been dating the cousin off and on but mostly off for 6 years. I can't seem to let her go. Is she the ghost shadow of my feelings for her cousins, for the one who made me whole and the one who broke me? It's the mother of these two old lovers who had died right about the time the crows harassed me with their calls; were they telling me of her passing away. Is she still angry with me for making her girls unhappy? It is 30 years ago, a lifetime that stole the younger sister and the grandmother so many moons ago, and now it was the mother. All that had happened was now between myself and Kresenzia. We were the two to outlast that angst and memories. So I asked after her.

"How is Kresenzia", I had lost touch with her decades ago in that period of young adult restlessness and doubt, in that period of grace. The best grace a human could ever have is restlessness and sadness. Poets understand this easily, they learn grace by mourning and playing with words. Words are art. Grace is art, Sadness is art. Restlessness is art. Doubt is art. Being the artist here is developing the ability to deal with that which wants to eat you by letting it consume you whole.

"She is fine. She stayed behind home after the funeral, receiving guests; she must have left home just a day ago."

"Where is she now staying?"

"She is staying in South Africa."

Later that night I go to sleep wondering why I had decided to get in touch with the cousin when I had ended it over a year ago. Was it to learn about my first lover's mum- her passing away? I am sad, wounds I thought I had cased inside feel like they had happened yesterday. That night I broke, like a torn map!

We never really heal, do we? We never stop loving them, do we? We just face forward as we learn to live without them, even though we still fester silently.

I don't want to say sorry because I will be apologizing for being me. Who would I be if not me? It's hard to live everyday with who I am, but it's what I know. I know this is a walk that never seem to end, walking through the cartography of your cruelty.

Of course I am sorry about her death, the pain it caused my first lover. She was her mother in my own mother.

Tomb of the Unknown Soldier
David Chasumba

Tererai was kneeling and weeding the grass between the black granite gravestones at the Heroes Acre cemetery. It was a week before the Heroes Day celebrations and two weeks before the Presidential elections. He turned around and saw a man holding a wreath and standing in front of the tomb of the Unknown Soldier. The man gazed up at the statue and placed the wreath at the foot of the statue. He stepped back and saluted.

He stood up and approached the man. He cleared his throat.

The man jolted back to reality and turned around.

'Good morning, sir?' Tererai smiled at the tall, smartly dressed, middle-aged man.

The man smiled a friendly smile. 'I'm Moses. And you?'

'Tererai. I am a gardener and general hand here. Pleased to meet you, sir.' He shook Moses' hand.

'Pleased to meet you too, Tererai.'

'Do you live here, in Harare?'

'Yes and no. I have a home here in Harare, but I live in a small quiet town, Bexhill-on-sea in England.'

'I could tell from your fluent English accent that you come from the diaspora.'

'Thank you.'

'We don't normally see people from the diaspora, come here and lay a wreath at the tomb of the Unknown Soldier. I hope you don't mind me asking, but what brings you here, to this tomb of the Unknown Soldier?'

'My Uncle Lovemore, the eldest son of my mother's brother, a ZANLA combatant died during the war of liberation, fighting for the freedom of the black people of this country.'

'When did he join the war?'

'1976.'

'Where did your uncle come from?'

'A village near Katiyo in Uzumba Maramba Pfungwe.'

'I heard that there were fierce battles between the ZANLA forces and the Rhodesian army there.'

'Yes. The ZANLA forces operated in my uncle's village with the support of the povo- people of various opinions. But the Rhodesian government responded by creating protected villages, Keeps, fenced and guarded villages to protect the villagers from feeding the 'terrorists', the ZANLA forces. The villagers lived under a 6pm curfew and had to show an ID to leave or return to the protected village before the curfew. One could easily be shot and killed if you didn't produce the ID. They were suspected of being 'terrorists'. The Ian Smith government didn't want the villagers supporting the terrorists.'

'How long did your uncle live in these protected villages?'

'Two years.'

'How did he end up being involved in the war then?'

'Uncle Lovemore was tortured by the Rhodesian forces when a sellout told them that he was still collaborating with the terrorists as a *Chimbwido*. After the torture, he fled with his family to our home in Sinoia, present day Chinhoyi.'

'Why did they flee to Sinoia?'

'The cities and towns were safer than rural villages and were refuge for displaced rural families.'

'What was your relationship with your uncle Lovemore like?'

'I loved him a lot. He was in his late teens. He loved to tell stories; folk tales, *Ngano* and other stories about living in the protected villages. He had seen villages bombed and razed to the ground, villagers killed, and dead combatants displayed in public to scare villagers from joining the terrorists. He produced model cars out of wire. I loved driving my wire model car on the dusty streets of the high-density township of Chitambo, Chinhoyi. Many times, Uncle Lovemore carried me on his back, and we went to the shops. He also liked courting girls. My dad owned a small grocery shop and was generous to his in-laws who were suffering from post-traumatic stress disorder.'

'And what happened next?'

'Unbeknown to my family, Uncle Lovemore began sneaking out of the house and hanging out with other teenagers at a certain house in Chitambo township. Black townships were recruitment centres for the freedom fighters.'

'Oh no!'

'Uncle Lovemore was radicalized to join the war and take arms to fight the Ian Smith government. He was noticeably quiet and was no longer as friendly. He no longer talked about girls. I wanted to ask what the matter was, but he had withdrawn into himself. One day, I followed him from a distance. I saw him shake hands with strange looking youths of his age and he disappeared behind a certain house. I wanted to call him back. I wish to this day that I should have told my mother what Uncle Lovemore was up to.'

'The following day, Uncle Lovemore took me to the shops as usual. He bought me a candy cake. He told me that he loved me a lot. He put a letter in my back pocket and told me to give my mother in the evening. He told me he was going somewhere, and he would be back soon. He left me by the gate and walked away. That was the last time I saw my dear Uncle Lovemore.'

Tears streamed out of Moses' eyes.

'Later in the evening, my worried mother asked me if I knew where Uncle Lovemore was. I said no. My mum went out looking for him in the houses of some of his friends in the township. My mum was distraught when she returned home and there was no sign of him. He was always home on time. Late at night I remembered the letter that he had put in my back pocket.'

Moses took out a discolored envelope and handed the worn-out letter to Tererai. 'This is the letter that he wrote 47 years ago.'

The letter was barely legible and read:

145

Dear Tete and family

I have decided to join the war of liberation and fight for the freedom of my black people. I have observed the way black people have been oppressed under the Smith regime. I hated living in the protected village, in Keep, like an animal in my own ancestral land. I couldn't just hide from the war in the sanctuary of the towns and cities. I made up my mind to fight for freedom. If it is God's wish that we should unite one day, in an independent country, so be it. But if I should die fighting to liberate my country, please don't mourn me forever. I gave my precious life for the freedom of future generations. I was not coerced into joining the war of liberation. I joined out of free will. I joined fellow comrades to free out mother land, Zimbabwe. I will always love you. Pass my warm regards to little Moses.

I will always love you,

Lovemore.

Moses smothered tears. 'My mother and the whole family cried for days and wished they had known what Uncle Lovemore was up to and stopped him. But there was nothing we could do. Many youths were recruited by ZANLA that way. The family at the home where Uncle Lovemore went said they had never seen him. I am sure they knew all about him, but they didn't want to admit it. It was an offence to not report that a family member had joined the war of liberation. The BSAP would have visited our home and arrested my parents. Everyone kept silent those days. You didn't know if your neighbour was a sellout.'

'Did he return from the war?'

'It's a long story. After the ceasefire and the ongoing Lancaster House talks, the combatants left the battlefield for the assembly points. It was a time of joy and sorrow. Families reunited with their loved ones who had been fighting in the bush. Some members grieved their loved ones that they had lost in the war. The assembly points were dangerous places where the war hardened combatants were suspicious of the ongoing talks and were itching to return to the bush to fight. My mum and her brother, Uncle Chirenje, Lovemore's father, visited different assembly points. They returned frustrated that they didn't see Uncle Lovemore. They held onto the thread of hope that one day Uncle Lovemore would walk back home. They asked everywhere but none of the combatants remembered Uncle Lovemore. The hope of finding him alive faded every day. He didn't return home. My family wanted closure.'

'So, what happened then?'

Moses looked up in the sky and sobbed. He avoided eye contact with Tererai. 'Then in 1981 a disabled stranger with crutches walked into the yard of our home in Sinoia, now renamed Chinhoyi. At first, I thought it was Uncle Lovemore but realized that this man looked older and shorter. I was disappointed. The stranger introduced himself to my mother and father as the commander of the section that Uncle Lovemore and other combatants belonged to. He described Uncle Lovemore as a brave freedom fighter. He narrated the tragic story of the section that he commanded.

***

The ZANLA freedom fighters had regularly raided remote grocery shops and looted for food, clothes, and other provisions. But on one fateful day, they raided a white owned rural grocery store. But unbeknown to them there was an observation point of Rhodesian forces on top of a nearby mountain. The observers had spotted them and radioed back up. The backup had responded quickly.

On the way out of the grocery shop with loot, the comrades were fired at from helicopters and quickly surrounded by ground troops parachuting from helicopters. There was a gunfire. The comrades were outnumbered and outgunned. Five of the nine comrades were killed on the scene. Uncle Lovemore had survived the shooting. He and four of his comrades were captured and taken away.

It was the routine for the triumphant Rhodesian forces to display the dead bodies of the comrades and warn the villagers that such fate would befall them if they joined the 'terrorists'. None of the villagers knew where the dead bodies were buried.

Uncle Lovemore was taken to hospital for treatment. He was guarded on his hospital bed. After he got better, he was taken to a detention camp where he was tortured for information. His interrogators wanted to know where the freedom fighters' bases were located, the weapons that they had in their arsenal, their operations, and military tactics and how they received provisions from outside the country.

But Uncle Lovemore refused to talk and sell out his comrades. They continued to torture him and try to turn him. He saw the section commander during the torture. He told him about his torture. He gave him my mum's address in Sinoia. Uncle Lovemore had died during the torture and his body was dumped at an unknown location.

The section commander had feigned cooperation with the Rhodesian forces. He miraculously escaped captivity and rejoined the comrades. He had expected to reunite with Uncle Lovemore at the nearby assembly point, after the ceasefire. But they didn't meet. He said that Uncle Lovemore was a gallant freedom fighter.

My mum broke down and cried. I went inside the house. It was now filled with loud crying. It was a bittersweet closure for the family.

Weeks later my family went to our rural village to carry out the Shona cultural traditions and rituals to bring Uncle Lovemore's 'wandering spirit back home'. According to Shona tradition Uncle Lovemore's dead spirit was wandering in the jungle. It needed to be brought back home and be appeased. A grave for Uncle Lovemore was erected in his village.

***

'I am really sorry to hear about the tragic story of your Uncle Lovemore. I always wondered what the tomb of the Unknown Soldier really stood for.'

'It pays homage to the gallant freedom fighters, dead and alive, including my Uncle Lovemore, who paid the ultimate sacrifice to liberate this country.'

'Fair enough. I respect the ultimate sacrifices that your uncle Lovemore and many more freedom fighters made to free the country. But look at the current state of the country; high level of corruption, the high unemployment, the brain drain, the suppression of freedom of speech, and incarceration without trial of opposition party members like Job Sikhala, the looting of the nation's resources shown in the Gold Mafia documentary and many more problems bedeviling the country.'

'It is clear that the country is facing challenges that have also been worsened by the sanctions that affected economic development. What has this to do with my Uncle Lovemore?'

'He and other freedom fighters fought for freedom. But we are not eating the fruits of that freedom. Look I have a BA degree in Shona Language and work here at the Heroes Acre as a gardener and general hand. Don't I deserve a chance to get a good job, without paying someone corrupt, to get employment? Didn't your Uncle Lovemore die that we could live in a country full of milk and honey?'

'Yes. I have sympathy for you, Tererai, for the problems you are experiencing in the country. I don't have a right to lecture you on who you should vote for in the upcoming elections, when I live in the diaspora. That is your constitutional right.'

'I won't vote for these corrupt leaders. I will vote for change. It was high time there was change in this country.'

'You are entitled to hold your opinion and vote for anyone who you think brings the change that you want. But it doesn't take away the fact that my Uncle Lovemore and other gallant fighters, immortalized by this tomb of the Unknown Soldier, died so that you could exercise that constitutional right. It is up to you whether you want to vote to safeguard the sacrifices and gains of liberation or as you say, you want to vote for change.'

'I will definitely vote for change.'

'Good day, and good luck, Tererai.'

He watched Moses walk away. He felt sympathy for him. He lived abroad but carried the deep scars of a long-forgotten war. Maybe Moses was right that the younger generation must not take for granted the hard-won gains of independence. But what was there to celebrate in this wasteland, where his dreams are differed?

Tererai imagined that Moses' Uncle Lovemore might have been an old man with children and grandchildren now. He felt his pain. He realized that every generation has its own problems. The previous generation fought hard for independence. But his generation was fighting a different struggle against the liberators who had become repressive. All he wanted was to enter the voting booth and vote for change. But would the change that he craved for materialize? He wasn't sure. At least he had a better understanding why other people still voted for the ruling party, despite and still, the problems in the country. He returned to his weeding.

Hustling - the daily struggle in Harare
Hosea Tokwe

July 2024

Piyo threw away the blankets from his springy bed alarmed by the intense brightness of the light spreading in his room. He hurriedly put on his black track suit bottom with yellow stripes and a grey tshirt. Retrieving his dirty canvas shoes underneath the bed he cursed himself for being late again knowing full well that this was a big blow to his meagre budget. To make matters worse for the third time he was wearing the same clothes again. How demeaning. But there was nothing he could do to improve his looks and outlook. The populace had become impoverished and he was not spared either. In today's fast life of hustling no one bothered to ask anybody's dressing and sense of decorum. How Piyo had fitted into this kind of life went without question. Life moved on.

Piyo checked his wrist watch once again. Surely, by now it was too late catching the much cheaper transport. He had nobody to blame but himself for his troubles.

He now stood up thinking deeply as he reflected on the long journey that he had traveled. A journey of hardship in a country whose economic meltdown had become the talk of the region, where struggling people came face to face with debilitating poverty.

Since completing his higher secondary school studies, Piyo had not secured a place at any of the local Universities neither could he afford the fees. His mother despite working at a government institution had openly advised him that she could not afford the tuition fees. For three months he had tried to post his curriculum vitae to different companies, sending unsolicited applications without success. Thus, when one day he met an older schoolmate who advised him to order trinkets for resale in the city centre.

'Jeffrey do you think this will work out', Piyo asked his friend as he caressed his mineral bottle.

'Mmmmmm yaah' Jeffrey mumbled after taking another bit of the seasoned chicken slice piece.

'You can give it a try for two months and come back to me', Jeffrey assured his friend his searching eyes gazing at him.

Piyo shied away nodding his head good-naturedly more out of acknowledging his friend's encouragement.

As they enjoyed their food at this Chicken Inn outlet Piyo listened attentively to Jeffrey's sojourn to Dubai as he recounted the several trips that he had taken to secure orders for bales of clothing, and different types of trinkets. There was the hustling to secure visa and last-minute air tickets purchases and flight bookings. Dubai to most people in African countries had become the gateway to the Middle East countries. The big business people were now into trading in fuel from some oil producing countries.

Piyo had listened to his friend imagining how great it would be to one day seize the opportunity to fly out to Dubai. But today he had to contend with his lateness.

Piyo jumped into a high roof commuter omnibus just a few moments before it took off at this popular intersection of the neighbourhood location. As the speeding commuter bus headed towards the bridge, Piyo raised his eyes to get a better view of the landing airline. No, this was not the Emirates Airlines he had thought but the South African Airways preparing to land on the runway. Each time they passed adjacent to the runaway a piece of his mind always reflected on the Dubai story.

Fumbling his pockets, he felt for his torn purse. For a fraction of a second his heart lept with panic, but he relaxed moments later. In haste he had thrown the purse inside the paperback that he now held on his lap. That he now remembered. So from the very purse he now pulled out a dirty United States one dollar note and forwarded it to the conductor. Patiently he waited for his change.

Not long there were in bustling and hustling of the city. Wriggling his way through the mass of human traffic he gritted his teeth with anger at the obstructing people all driven to the city by the quest to survive. Shoulders brushed roughly on each other, others stamped on each other's feet rushing their apologies in the confusing movements.

On the intersection, the traffic officer summoning all bags of tricks fought hard to control the traffic jungle.

Piyo's mouth went agape. He had been late and today his selling post was already occupied. Stamping his feet in anger he waited agonizingly for the late arrival of Mr. Patel from where he had left his trinkets the previous day. Around him tongue lashing voices could be heard echoing and competing all in an effort to win customers. Individualism had gripped young men, women and the elderly all in an effort to survive

'The Cult of the Hustle' all centred on going on it alone, being your own boss had addicted all the populace for through encouragement right from the family, church and community everybody felt being an entrepreneur in his or her right. Piyo found himself in the thick of this dog eat dog affair.

'Municipal police!', a piercing voice shouted from nowhere. That voice was enough to alert all. Suddenly the street vendors took to their heels in different directions. Amid the fleeing trinkets and fruits were strewn in the tarmac as vendors escape in different directions in an effort to avoid arrest. This time they had been smart, though some of their trinkets and fruits were strewn all over the tarmac others had quickly hidden in bale shops. The battle had been briefly won, Municipal truck swept past loaded with heavily armed men wilding rubber baton sticks.

From a street corner Piyo stared his heartbeat pounding heavily. His last fear was being jailed. No, he did not like to take any further chances. He had one idea in mind, to return back home.

Pains of a Widowed bride
Tanea Nyika

As the dawn of 18 November broke, with a few sun's rays streaming in through my rusted windows casting a soft glow across my room, I suddenly regretted being born. There I was sitting alone, just as how I came into this world, alone, in my favorite rocking armchair, moving but going nowhere. Alone, as I'd been my whole life and my mind racing with the same pace of the chair but still, just like the chair, going nowhere.

Deep inside I've always had that haunting sadness, my mind, a tumultuous sea of memories and emotions, each wave crashing against the shores of my consciousness, leaving behind fragments of pain and regret. Deep down I'd always known that the devil will catch on to me and that thought could never allow me to settle or hope for any better future. The weight of my sorrows always seemed to hang in the air, suffocating me with its heaviness but that morning as I gazed out the window at the gentle, golden hues of the sunrise, I knew that I was about to live the events of the day that would shatter my world. The day the devil would finally get his claims. Again and again I tried to escape the reality of this wedding with what I'd known of him but the dilemma as always, had me on it's horns. I vividly recall the day all my respect, love and admiration for him came falling down just as how the diamond pieces of the other necklace he'd bought me had also fallen down after he stripped it away from my neck with all his might for simply denying him one night.

The day is still etched in my memory with unforgiving clarity, a day that had left me heartbroken and adrift in a sea of despair, the day that had left me in this desolate moment of solitude and sorrow on a day that was supposed to make me the merriest, a day I'd forever planned and rearranged as a girl. All dreams were shuttered by the truth that the devil for once allowed me to see that early morning as I was on my usual morning jog. As a passed by my fiance's house, the young, affluent Mayor named Byron, I decided to stop by and retrieve my puppy that the nanny had been looking after for me the previous day. I noticed the main door standing ajar and, receiving no response to my calls, I decided to enter the house.

After a while of yelling 'Pitzy, Pitzy', I heard what I assumed was a bit of moaning coming from the slightly ajar bedroom door. Assuming it was Pitzy, I ventured into the room assuming that Byron was on his work trip as he'd said. The room was filled with utter darkness and slowly, I opened the door like the mechanism of a spring loaded gun afraid that Pitzy might sneak out before I noticed. Blindly, I searched on the walls for a bulb switch for the light. As soon as the lights were on, I met the utter horror of all horrors in my life. On the bed was a naked brunette and my fiance. Caught between anger, pain, and a lingering love for the man that stood before me, I started shivering uncontrollably as the cold chill slowly swept over my spine. Finally some words found their way out of my throat. "I need time," I remember I'd said in a slight whisper as my eyes searched his for any sign of sincerity. "Time to understand, time to heal, time to decide." I'd added. The silence in the room was so deafening, broken only by the sound of my own racing heartbeat and a distant crack of the bed as he went back to sitting down. There and then I knew I wasn't going to be granted any time as I'd bravely said but rather, it was the time for unending threats and bribes to promise that I wouldn't shame him and indeed that afternoon the threats began the same way he'd done to get me agreeing to marry him.

Indeed the shock of the scene had left me paralyzed and unable to comprehend the devastation that had unfolded before my eyes. The man I was about to vow my life to, had shattered my trust and broken my heart in the cruelest of ways. As I stumbled out of the house that day, the weight of betrayal and disbelief clung to me like a heavy cloak, and the world around me blurred as tears stung my eyes then freely breaking into two thin streams down my cheeks, just like that, on the

18th of November as I waited for the cars to start arriving. As soon as they did, I ran to the bathing room. I allowed myself a good sip in the bathtub as the warm water blended with my tears. The weight of the day ahead was already bearing down on me. The sound of laughter and chatter from the arriving guests filtered through the walls, a stark contrast to the turmoil within my heart, even now. Each moment of joy and celebration would be a cruel reminder of the pain and uncertainty that now defined my love story. With the knowledge that I'd to go in front of people and look strong I let out the last sobs with a depth of emotion that threatened to consume me. The echoes of my cries filled the room, a symphony of grief and longing for the love and trust I had once believed in. The once bright vision of my wedding day then felt like a distant dream, replaced by the harsh reality of a fractured heart and a future shrouded in doubt.

Wiping away my tears, the resolve in my eyes cut through the despair. Standing up, I looked at myself in the mirror, a silent promise forming in my heart. The day indeed had started with tears, but I tried to refuse to let it end in defeat which was in all ways inevitable. Then again I reasoned with myself as to why I'd chosen to wed in November, a month highly known for misfortunes but well November or no November, one's character wouldn't change. With a deep breath, I gathered my strength to step out of the bathroom but couldn't. I wasn't ready to face the day and the uncertain future that lay beyond it. The sound of the approaching celebration grew louder, but within me, a quiet strength began to take hold, a flicker of resilience amidst the storm. As the gentle but persistent knocking on the bathroom door continued, a flurry of activity unfolded outside. His sisters were so eager to support and the makeup artists, determined to make me look my best. A lot of exchanges cheerfully went on and compliments about the grandeur of my impending marriage to the mayor. Yet, within the cocoon of my thoughts, I grappled with the weight of my inner turmoil.

With each step toward the chair and each brush of makeup against my skin, I felt the weight of their well-intentioned words. The facade of privilege and prestige that surrounded my impending marriage to the mayor felt suffocating, a gilded cage that threatened to confine my spirit. The whispers of envy and admiration from the dressers only served to deepen the chasm between the reality I faced and the illusion of happiness that the world saw. As I looked at my reflection in the mirror, the weight of expectations and appearances went down on me more and more. The knots in my stomach tightened with each passing moment, my heart heavy with the knowledge that my so-called "luck" came at a steep price. The words of congratulations and admiration rang hollow in my ears, even now they still do, a stark contrast to the ache of uncertainty and fear that defined my reality. In the midst of the whirlwind of preparations, a quiet resolve managed to take root within me. Beneath the layers of makeup and the opulent gown, I still carried the burden of a truth that could not be concealed. Despite the facade of privilege and admiration, I knew that my journey ahead was fraught with challenges and sacrifices that no amount of grandeur could mask.

Stepping out of the car, the grandeur of the cathedral and the overwhelming festivities enveloped me in a wave of sound and color.

The jubilant cacophony of car horns, ululations, and laughter filled the air, a testament to the spectacle that the wedding had become.

Multitudes from all walks of life had gathered, their eyes alight with curiosity and excitement, eager to witness the union of two prominent figures. Amidst the sea of faces, the groom stood at the altar, resplendent in his immaculate tuxedo, a picture of confidence and anticipation. As I made my entrance, I was so grateful for the veil which concealed a torrent of tears as the crowd murmured in hushed admiration of my prison, probably mistaking my emotions for the expected display of sentimentality on such a momentous occasion.

Beneath the veil, my tears flowed unchecked, a silent testament to the tumult of emotions that threatened to consume me now and again. The weight of expectation and obligation hung heavy on my shoulders, the grandeur of the cathedral a stark reminder of the suffocating opulence that had come to define my existence. All that while, I longed to shatter the illusion of joy and celebration, to scream out the truth that lay concealed beneath the layers of tradition and spectacle. I wish I'd betrayed him just as in the days of Hitler when those little kids spilled all the truth about their parents, I wish I had.

Walking down the aisle, the weight of my tears mingled with the weight of the ornate gown. The world around me saw a bride immersed in the emotion of the moment, but within me, a storm raged, a tempest of defiance and resignation, a silent scream for freedom and authenticity. As I reached the altar, Byron's eyes met mine, a mask of joy and expectation veiling the truth that lay between us. In the stillness of the cathedral, amidst the opulence and grandeur, I stood at the precipice of a life-altering decision, but could only give out tears, a silent plea for understanding and liberation.

Stopping in my tracks, the world around me seemed to blur, the weight of the moment amplified by the unexpected sight of my ex. The badge displayed prominently on his chest, identifying him as a member of the Mayor's security team, which added a surreal layer of complexity to an already tumultuous situation. In that singular moment, the past and the present collided, and the truth I'd sought to bury surged to the surface. The presence of my ex, then entwined with the grandeur of the cathedral and the prominence of the occasion, felt like a cruel twist of fate, a reminder of the tangled web of connections and obligations that bound me.

As our eyes met, a myriad of unspoken emotions swirled between us, a silent exchange that transcended the weight of the present moment. Byron, unaware of the charged atmosphere that lingered in the air, stood beside me, his gaze filled with anticipation and joy. Yet, in the depths of my heart, a maelstrom of conflicted emotions threatened to engulf me and if it be possible, even choke me to death. As the cathedral stood to witness the grandeur and tradition of the occasion, I stood at the crossroads of my destiny. As the wedding ceremony reached the pivotal moment of exchanging rings, a hushed anticipation filled the cathedral. All eyes being fixed on us, immersed in the solemnity of the occasion. However, amidst the reverent silence, a figure walked purposefully down the aisle, his imposing presence unnoticed in the midst of the congregation's focus on the groom and I.

Heavily built and bearing a steely resolve in his expression, the intruder moved with a singular determination, a silent force that disrupts the veneer of celebration and tradition. Unnoticed by the assembled guests, his presence stood as a stark contrast to the grandeur and opulence.

In the midst of the charged atmosphere, the figure reached the altar, his presence was such a disruptive force that cast a shadow over the ceremony. The weight of his unspoken intentions loomed large. The unexpected arrival of the enigmatic figure became a harbinger of uncertainty, a disruption that pierced through the facade of the celebrations In the stillness of the moment, a silent question hung in the air, threatening to shatter the illusion of joy and unity that the wedding sought to embody. Just then I noticed the same badge as he pulled down his face mask. The sudden and jarring sight of the intruder brandishing a pistol, his intent unmistakable as he targeted the mayor, sent shock waves of panic and disbelief through the cathedral. In an instant, the solemnity of the occasion gave away to a scene of chaos and fear. "You won't get to abuse that power, son." The words hung right under the expected sound of the bullet that hit straight through Byron's chest. Falling to the ground with him in my arms all I could see was the blood which was oozing profusely onto my gown.

The gasps and cries of the gathered guests filled the air in that harrowing moment, a cacophony of alarm and confusion reverberating through the once serene space. Turning to my right, I saw my ex still seated as he was when I walked in with a smirk on his once handsome face. I wished that I could rip him apart but he'd given back a small piece of revenge and I knew there was definitely more.

Pieces of Wood
Matthew K Chikono

The foot tall maize plants were turning yellow in the scorching sun and I knew by the end of the week we were going to lose the entire crop; it meant another year of getting by. Not once had it rained the entire month of November.

I wiped sweat from my forehead with the back of my hand. Weeding was exhausting, worse whilst choking on the dust raised by hoes hitting the dry earth. The burning sensation of an empty stomach reminded me that I could faint if I didn't take a break. Beside me, my grandfather wiped his nose. He didn't seemed to sweat but I knew he was struggling as much as I was. He was in his mid-seventies and that kind of work was now decades behind him.

I stood up for a moment to stretch my back. My eyes glided across the one acre field we were farming. It was surrounded by many others of the same size belonging to our fellow Chisi villagers. However, it was the only one with maize, a crop not suitable in our particular region. My grandfather noticed me eyeing our pending doom.

"Don't worry Tigere," he said," It will work, we have done exactly what Hubert Carlos did at his farm."

Hubert Carlos was a white farmer my grandfather had worked for in the seventies. My grandfather claimed that the farmer had grown maize in a more hot and arid condition than we had in Chisi. My grandfather had convinced me to follow this farmer's method and plant maize for that season, he was sure it would succeed. It now seemed the promised bumper harvest would not suffice.

My grandfather continued tilling the ground. His voice, between the heavy breathing, started narrating all the marvelous and miraculous farming that white man had done. He continued telling me about his own life and work at the farm. My grandfather recalled and narrated his younger days when his life seemed hard. It made his less sad. I let him tell the story again.

We decided to take a break from the weeding. It was almost noon and we had to eat our lunch. We sat under the trees at the edge of the field and started eating mangai; a boiled salted seed mixture of maize, groundnuts and cowpeas. We shared a bottle of maheu which we sipped to make the food swallow easily.

After our lunch was done we continued with the weeding. From the corner of my eyes I could see the old man panting. He was exhausted.

"You should go home and rest now Sekuru," I offered, "I can manage alone."

"No Tigere." The man wheezed, "I am still capable."

I didn't insist, afraid to wound his already fragile pride. He didn't want to be seen as a declining old man. He kept pace with me until my own back started to hurt. Fortunately, we finished the entire field a couple of hours before sundown. We did not linger to admire our handwork, but went straight home.

We didn't have any cattle that needed to be herded home from the communal grazing lands at the end of the day. It made him sad, my grandfather, that he was now an old man without a single cow to his name. Neither a single goat nor a rooster to call his own. Each and every year he had relied on miracles to survive on the little that he harvest on his field. The little money I made from doing odd jobs in other people's fields bought cooking oil and salt in the house.

What he had was a home. Acres of farmland surrounding three thatched huts. The effects of time were visible on the walls of muddy huts. What used to be a chicken run was now a single waist level wall. The blair toilet stood proud on the leeway side. A pit was all that was left of the kraal that used to snuggle in a dozen or so cattle he owned during his prime. The three dilapidated huts, a toilet and a well was all he had now.

It was in one of the huts that we went in, kicked our sandals off, and put our feet up in the air just for a little while before we started preparing supper. I took some dried wood outside and put on a fire inside the kitchen. In a minute the whole hut was filled with smoke. I dashed outside in order to catch a breath of fresh air and bumped into a body.

"Good evening Tigere," the man said, "Is Sekuru Jemusi around?"

The mentioning of his name made my grandfather spring to his feet and rush to the door to see who was looking for him. There was a look of contempt on his face when he realised it was our neighbor, Zuze, who was asking about him. My grandfather hated Zuze, he claimed Zuze conspired with other witches in the village and killed his first wife.

"Good evening Sekuru Jemusi," Zuze said, "There's a donor at our church giving out food parcels to the elderly next Tuesday. Send Tigere with your ID card to register. I have already registered myself and now I am telling all my fellow neighbours to do the same."

Zuze didn't wait for my grandfather to reply. He started walking slowly towards his own homestead. Zuze loved his neighbor, enough to tell him about food parcels despite knowing fully that the neighbour hated him. My grandfather was sure that his stance at a local missionary church was a rouse to distract people from finding out how deep he was into witchcraft.

I watched Zuze walk away, he was as old as my grandfather. If my grandfather's accusations were true, then I owed my existence to that man. Without him killing my grandfather's first wife, my grandfather would have never married Marujata who bore my father.

My grandfather went back into the kitchen and sat on the stone bench. I followed him and sat beside the fire, stirring my pot.

"I have been reduced to this," the man started," my enemies feel pity for me, that they help me to find alms from strangers. How did my life come to this?"

I didn't have to answer. I didn't even look in his direction, I couldn't bear to see tears on his face. The man had five children with his first wife none who had visited him in over a decade. His second wife had borne him two sons neither had left home. The eldest, who was my father, comfortably rested in the family burial grounds whilst the younger son was somewhere in the village getting drunk to whatever he could lay his hands upon.

"Promise me Tigere," the old man sobbed," that you will bury me when I am dead. Promise me you will only abandon me after death. You are the last of my family you know that right?"

I continued stirring the pot murmuring something about him rumbling nonsense and needing rest. I thought I heard the old man cry but I couldn't make myself look. Later, I dished him sadza and dried kapenta.

"We are not eating together Tigere?"

"No grandfather," I replied, "I am going to the well to fetch some drinking water and I will eat when I come back."

I took a quick glance at the old man, he was struggling to chew with the few remaining teeth in his mouth. I slipped into the evening, leaving the empty bucket behind.

I took brisk steps towards the Msasa tree which stood tall and proud near the cattle dip tank. I found the two sisters waiting patiently. The younger sister started slowly walking away as soon as she saw me approaching.

"Why does your sister hate me that much?" I asked the older sister.

"I told you Tigere," Eustancia said,"Lukia is extremely shy."

Eustancia gave me a quick hug whilst her sister was looking away before breathing in my ear,"I missed you."

"How will she be able to bear it when I marry you and become her brother-in-law?" I asked.

"You shouldn't joke about marriage like that Tigere."

"I am serious," I said, "I want to marry you Eustancia."

"Then marry me tomorrow Tigere," Eustancia continued, "If you can't afford it, my aunt can help me elope in the evening."

I left her words hanging in the night air. The moon was slowly rising and a handful of stars were already tingling in the sky. Eustancia and I had been in love for a couple of months but I hadn't noticed how she was such in a hurry to get married to me.

"Listen Eustancia," I said, "you are still eighteen, there is no need to rush."

I went on explaining to her that before I could take her to my home I had to make a little money to support the family we were going to have. At that moment, I was struggling caring for my grandfather. I promised her only a couple of months were needed for me to go to the city and work it out.

"How are you going to find work in Harare?" She asked.

"I have been in contact with my aunt, my father's half-sister, she said I could live with her whilst I sort it out."

"What about your grandfather?" Eustancia asked, "who will take care of him during the time you are gone?"

I didn't answer, I didn't know the answer. My mind went back to earlier that evening when the old man had made me promise him not to leave him until his death. Odd how my future depended on the promise I didn't make.

"Lukia let's go home," Eustancia finally said, "Goodbye Tigere, we should get going if we ever want to reach home before midnight."

"My fault, I came late today," I said grabbing her hand, "my grandfather was talking a lot about his life, I couldn't leave him talking to himself."

"Your grandfather tells you a lot about his life," Eustancia said, "maybe you should write a book about him and call it leaflets of life or something."

I chuckled. One day, when we had started seeing each other, I had told Eustancia I wanted to be a writer. I was impressed that she had remembered that. Maybe she was the one. Why did she desperately wanted to be with me that much? It didn't seem like she was in love with me or something.

"Bye Tigere," she said, letting go of me and holding her sister's hand at the same time walking away, "remember I won't wait for you forever."

I wished she had kissed me, it would have made her sister uncomfortable. Also it would have made me happy. Wasn't it what love was supposed to be? I started walking back home. Unbridled thoughts of raging my twenty three year old brain, not sure what my life was supposed to be.

I reached my grandfather's homestead. The fire from the kitchen wasn't visible from the outside and I thought that it had gone out. I picked up some dry logs and twigs and went inside. There was some still red charcoals on the fire place. I put on the twigs, blew on it, and the fire quickly ignited.

The illuminating fire showed my grandfather still sitting on the stone bench slumping weirdly on the wall, his unfinished plate of food on the floor.

"Why are you sitting in the dark grandfather?" I asked him.

The silence told me the answer I wasn't ready for. I didn't have to touch him to know what death felt like, I could smell it in the air. I stared at my grandfather, hoping to catch a glimpse of death who had taken him away from me.

THE LAST PARTY
Placidia Chiwita

I have never been a fan of parties. I can count the number of parties I attended in my life with a single hand. I can't exactly say what I dislike about parties. Maybe it's the crowds, or the loud music, maybe it's the forced socialisation with people I hardly know.

"We used to be troublemakers at school," Tanaka was saying at the front. "Every time there was noise and the back, the teachers knew that it was us."

I am at a party and the loud girl making a speech is my old friend. This party is different, I know everyone here. This is a party thrown specifically for me. Everyone gathered here today left their homes and came here for me. I feel kind of overwhelmed but happy, very happy.

Tanaka is still speaking and I laugh at what she is saying. It's all true. We really used to be close back in primary school. Ours was a classic enemies turned to friend's situation. She came in as a transfer student when we were in Grade 5. One look at her and I could tell she wasn't your typical transfer student, the ones who are meek and quiet, who slink silently into the background while observing to see where they would fit in. No, Tanaka was loud. A day in and she already had a band of followers. I envied her for that.

I was always quiet in school which is why I don't remember what happened for us to clash and almost fight. Quiet as I was, I still never backed away from a fight. We would have gotten in trouble if we had fought inside the school premises, so we made an appointment to fight outside the gate after school in a typical primary school student's way.

When school finished, I made my way out in my lonesome and sure enough, Tanaka and her band of followers were waiting for me outside.

Needless to say, the fight never happened and Tanaka and I became as thick as thieves since then. To make it even better, we were put in the same class for our Form 1. My family moved away end of that year and I lost contact with her. Over the years, I saw her maybe three times when I visited my old neighbourhood. Last I heard, she had moved overseas, which is why I was pleasantly surprised to see her at this party.

I feel a hand on my shoulder. I turn around and see Mrs Moyo, my very first boss. Come to think of it, I have never had a male boss in my life. She started that chain.

"It's good to see you baby," she says, pulling me into a hug.

She always called me baby even when I worked for her. It made it easy for me to call her mum, especially considering all her children are older than me. She looks good, though she has gained a lot of weight since I last saw her years ago. She used to be very strict about her weight, I guess not anymore. Seeing her like this, I realise I missed her.

"How is the family?" I ask.

She throws her head back and laughs, "Growing. Munashe now has 4 kids!"

"What?"

"I know!" she says.

Munashe is only a few months older than me, how does he have four kids and I have none? Wait a minute.

"With the same mother?" I ask.

"Three different mothers," she says with a shake of her head. That explains a lot, he always was a womaniser, he even tried his luck with me.

I still haven't forgotten the $500 she borrowed from me when business was low and she never returned it. I never struck up the nerve to ask and I am not about to do it now, her presence means so much more.

I spot my mother going around and interacting with the guests. Melody is with her. Sweet Melody. We became friends at university and after all these years, we are still tight. I had more friends back in varsity and when we graduated, we kept in touch for a while and then with time, as we took different career paths and some got married, the communication ceased. I understand distance often puts a strain on relationships but I don't understand friendships that end when one gets married. Girls are even advised to distance themselves from their single friends when they get married. I still understand the reason for that. Perhaps they thing that us single girls will corrupt the married ones. It's different with Kudzi, her marriage didn't affect our friendship at all.

Speaking of Kudzi, I hear her contagious laugh. She is huddled at the back with Nyasha. Whatever they are watching on that phone seems to be so funny, I can see Nyasha's shoulders begin to shake. I wonder if she still has that habit. Back at school, we all knew to stay out of Nyasha's arm reach whenever something funny was going on because she would hit you. Some habits are hard to drop so I observe and wait. Soon enough Nyasha's hand comes up and she hits Kudzi's shoulder.

Hard.

I crack up in laughter and the two of them look at me, Kudzi rubbing her shoulder and Nyasha wiping the tears of glee from her eyes. Those two girls, we became friends in 'A' level. We were a band of six and we used to sit at the corner of the class. We had so much fun back at school, just remembering those days makes me smile. From the sleepovers where we would spend the whole night watching Korean dramas instead of studying, to the prayer sessions at the school grounds. Those girls made my school days memorable. I lost touch with most of them as time passed, except Kudzi. She stuck around even when life landed us in different countries, even when she got married and had children naming me Godmother to her son. I can't believe I have known them for over 20 years. All six of the girls are here and my heart is almost bursting with joy.

Oh, there is Mr Marange, my Form 5 and 6 class teacher. Look at that white hair! I am glad to see he still looks fit. I remember when he saw me the first time as I was applying for 'A' level, he told me to study economics because I would be good at it. I didn't listen and instead favoured geography. I have since regretted that decision and my stubbornness. 'A' level geography kicked my ass people, it did me so bad! It did everyone bad but especially me! Imagine having two As and an E! Instead of the 14-15 'A' level points I was aiming for, I ended up with 11 points just because of geography. All my hopes to get sponsorships went down the drain. To make matters worse, economics had such a high pass rate, everyone I know had an A in economics. I mean even Rudo got a B and it was common knowledge that she wasn't the brightest in class. If only I had listened to Mr Marange, I would have gotten my 15 points.

Wait a minute, is that? Yes, it is. I ignore the pain and run to him.

"Sir!" I say as soon as I reach him. He gives me a bright smile and pulls me for a hug.

"Good to see you kiddo!" he says. Mr Nhau, my old Shona teacher at 'O' level. He is one of the people I always wanted to see before I die. I never saw him again ever since the time I collected my 'O' level results many years ago. Until now! I am happy I got a chance to see him. Our relationship had a rocky start. I don't know how I moved from being his most notorious student to being his best one. In his defence, maybe it was because my notoriety wasn't that bad. I mean, it was just a simple case of late-coming. I was always late to school and he was always on gate duty. The number of punishments I had to do because of this man. He ended up accepting that I will never be early for school and my lateness became a subject of laughter. Soon enough, he was looking out for me and sometimes even waited to hear how I found the exam he had set for us. He would never admit it but I know I was his favourite student.

Behind him is another former teacher of mine, Mr Murwira, and he is holding a copy of Sidney Sheldon's Doomsday Conspiracy. He used to teach at the school where I did my 'A' level. He didn't directly teach me, but we always clashed because of my late-coming. This late-coming habit started from way back, I don't know what happens, I wake up early to start preparing but still end up late. Anyway, we discovered our mutual love for reading one day as he was supervising our punishment and since then, he started lending me books to read. He had a Sidney Sheldon collection and that was the time I fell in love with that author's work, may his soul rest in peace.

"I have known Rufaro for the longest time," a male voice was saying. Now who could that be? I don't recognise that fat man standing at the front. I walk closer and .... Hell no! What is Tawanda doing here and who invited him? I look around and see my mother giggling into her hands. Of course, it was her, she is the only one who would find this funny.

"We were so tight back at a school," he was saying scratching his belly.

Make him stop.

"I thought we were going to get married…"

Can someone please get him off that stage!

Only my parents and my 'O' Level school mates find this funny. The rest of my guests are looking at him with a mixture of mingled curiosity and confusion. He used to be so handsome back at school, and I had a huge crush on him. Almost everyone knew that, then he had to go and break my heart by dating my friend. I remember that I locked myself in my room and cried for days. Where is the betrayer? Not here? Good. She knew I liked him and went ahead and dated him. She was clearly not loyal. I have no use for backstabbers in what remains of my life.

Looking at him now, I wonder what I found attractive about him. He isn't wearing his age well. Those red eyes, big belly, oh boy Tawanda has lost the plot, and his looks. I can tell underneath of that flesh and filth, there is a handsome man waiting to come out, if he just takes better care of himself and stop smoking whatever substance is reddening his eyes and blackening his lips.

Oh well. I almost feel sorry for him then I remember the reason everyone is gathered here, then I feel sorry for myself.

And is that…?

"It's good to see you Rufaro," he says.

OMG! What? How? When? Damn can my heart stop beating so fast? I should probably close my mouth too. He pulls me into a hug and he smells so divine. How did he grow from a scrawny little boy who was the smallest in the whole class, to this? He grew into his looks that's for sure. If I had known he would grow up to be this hot, I wouldn't have rejected him all those years ago. We would probably be married with a bunch of good-looking kids by now.

In my defence, I don't have the gift of foresight, I mean he literally reached up to my chest and was so bone thin back in high school. Now he is easily the tallest man here, that body shows he is good friends with the gym and that skin is showing that he has a good skin care routine. And that beard! Damn that well-trimmed beard looks so good on him. I wish I could turn back time, I even forget that I am dying for a minute.

"Close your mouth, a fly might just fly in," Laura whispers in my ear. I immediately close my mouth and swallow.

"When did you become so hot?" I ask. He looks shocked at my directness, then bursts out laughing, Laura giggling behind me. I suppose this is the moment when normal people would feel ashamed, not me. Shame has no space in my life at this juncture. I see a ring on his finger. So, he is married. It's a good thing he didn't bring his wife. I don't want to see the woman occupying what could have been my position.

"I agree, Roy you are serving the looks," Laura agrees.

"It's nice to see that you two haven't changed after all these years," he says with a chuckle. "And it's really good to see you again Rufaro," he says, pulling me into a hug and walks away. I turn to Laura with a mournful look on my face.

She laughs and pulls me into a hug, "Shh, it's okay to cry," she says. "It's okay to mourn for the love that could have been but never was because you lacked the foresight to see a hunk that was hiding behind that skinny boy. I understand friend."

I fake crying on her shoulder and that invites another fit of giggles from her. Laura was my high school friend and classmate. We got close because of our mutual love for Korean dramas, reading and writing. We kept in touch all through 'A' Level and reconnected when we went to the same university. We were tight for the first two years, then she became distant. My texts went unanswered, promises broken and calls unanswered. On a call that she did manage to pick up, I vented to her on how the friendship was one sided and it seemed like I was the one chasing after her. After that, I stopped.

She must have lost my number, or deleted it because I later heard she was looking for my number from a mutual friend. He didn't give it to her. It would be years later, when I had a lot of airtime that was almost expiring and no one to call, that I scrolled through my contacts and came across her name and called her. She was so happy! I could hear the joy in her voice on that call and she chastised me on having her number and not getting in touch at all those years. We kept in touch since then.

"And look who else is here," she says. "If it isn't your first real boyfriend."

I look and yes, it is him. Oh Chris. He looks good and he wears glasses now! I have good taste on men if I do say so myself. I smile as I stare at him, we might have broken up ages ago before we graduated but we had some good times. He was my first kiss too. What makes him so memorable is that he is the only guy who sat me down and told me exactly why we couldn't continue dating. I cried my eyes out and hated him for some time.

It was after continuously meeting men who chose to treat me like trash and go quiet on me instead of ending the relationship that I got to appreciate Chris. Ladies, a man who sits you down and talks to you about ending a relationship is noble! Appreciate him. Men these days extend a lot of energy in pursuing you but when they are done, they would rather treat you bad in hopes that you get the hint and end the relationship first, or else they just ghost you as if they aren't the ones who were blowing up your phone when they wanted you.

Oh, and there is Jeff! He flew all the way from Canada for this? I am so touched and I think I'm going to cry but I can't do that because all these people who are here for me and trying to be strong will cry too. I met Jeff at a summer program many years ago. We didn't meet again since that program ended, until now. What is he holding? He starts waving it at me and it's a miniature version of a rollercoaster ride. I throw my head back and laugh. This is so like him! We went to an amusement park during the program and I somehow ended up teamed with him. We went around the park trying out all sorts of rollercoaster rides, screaming like banshees on some of them, very dizzy on most and feeling exhilarated and wanting more after all of them. That was my first encounter with adrenaline rush and I loved it. That is a memory I kept close because I never went back to an amusement park since.

Oh, there is Hope and Hillary, the very first women to mentor me. Hope was my career mentor while Hillary was my spiritual mentor. These two women made a significant impact in my life and I will always be grateful to them. Hillary always cried easily and it's no surprise seeing her cry as she talks about my growth.

My parents come and sit on either side of me. I put my head on my father's shoulder and hold my mother's hand as I listen to Hillary speak. My parents made this possible, they came together with my friends and organised this amazing party for me. I don't know how they managed it, but they invited everyone who was important to me.

How they managed to remember everyone, I have no idea.

Everyone gathered here today was in my life for a season. These are the people who brought a smile to my face whenever I thought of them. Some of them left after that season had passed while others stuck around. I look around and spot Kudzi and Melody sitting at the back. They had become close friends because of their mutual friendship with me and it has been a joy to see.

What makes me happy is that everyone here knows the reason they are gathered here, they know I am dying, they know that this might as well be the last time they are seeing me alive but none of them are crying. They are looking at me with genuine joy at seeing me again, they are standing on that stage and speaking about what a good person I am and the impact I have had in their lives. They are bringing up long buried memories and thanking me for things I had long forgotten. Some of them even dug up old photographs that I had forgotten and

I got to laugh as I went through them.

Instead of writing statuses and long social media posts after I am gone and not able to see it, they are telling me their words now when I'm able to hear and appreciate them. They are saying goodbye to me while they still can. As much as I am in pain right now, and it hurts so bad, I am just happy that my illness managed to prepare my loved ones for my inevitable demise, it gave them a chance to say goodbye.

Death is no stranger to any of us. We don't often think of it, it's the one thing we all know is coming but we tend to ignore. In the times that we do think of it, we want it to be the quick, it has to be painless. Dying peacefully while sleeping is everyone's dream. I know it was mine.

The reasons for this are mostly selfish. No one wants a painful death. A visit to the hospital leaves most depressed. And then we tell ourselves it's because we don't want our loved ones to suffer. They will be plagued with hospital bills if I get sick for a prolonged period of time we say. I don't want them to see me waste away in pain we think.

But perhaps an illness, as much as it hurts, will prepare those remaining behind and give them closure. As much as we would prefer a sudden death, it tends to come as a shock to our loved ones and makes it difficult for them to accept and cope.

I have watched my parents and friends go through the five stages of grief. Denial when I was first diagnosed with Stage 4 stomach cancer.

"No, it can't be! There has to be a mistake. How come we never saw it?" they said.

Anger as they saw the cancer eat away at me. The pain, the retching, not being able to keep anything down.

"Why is this happening to you? Why is God letting this happen to my daughter? Why her?" they said.

Then came the bargaining, begging the doctors please save me, begging God to heal me, attending all night prayers, fasting and climbing mountains.

Depression when they saw no change, as I continued to get more and more frail, as the cancer spread and the times where I had to be rushed to the hospital in the middle of the night because of the amount of pain I was in.

And finally, acceptance that their little girl was on her way out, that they weren't going to spend Christmas with her. They made a decision to make my final days as comfortable as possible and also make the best of what little time they had with me.

I worry about them, how are they going to cope when I'm gone? I always told them to have more children but they kept insisting that I was enough. If I had siblings, I wouldn't have to worry so much about their well-being after I'm gone. Now they are going to be left alone. Had I not been so career oriented, I might have settled down and given them grandchildren. That way they would always have a part of me even after I am gone.

When death is calling, it puts a lot of things into perspective. You start rewinding your life like a cassette and thinking what you could have done better and I will tell you now as someone who is going through it. What I regret the most are the birthdays I missed, the harsh words I once uttered, the time I wasted pursuing meaningless things, the times when my pride prevented me from contacting my loved ones, the relationships I let go of and the places I didn't get to visit. It's not the money I think of these days or the job but the relationships, because at the end of the day, the people in your life are what matters.

I am grateful that I got a chance to reconnect with most of them before I die. Looking at them gathered here, eating, dancing and laughing brings me joy. They will probably cry at my funeral but now, right now all I see are people who are happy to see me.

This is indeed the best funeral anyone have ever gotten. It is the best party I have ever attended; it is also my last party.

Mmap Fiction and Drama Series

If you have enjoyed *Zimbolicious 10th Anniversary Anthology: New and Collected Fictions* consider these other fine books in **Mmap Fiction and Drama Series** from *Mwanaka Media and Publishing*:

The Water Cycle by Andrew Nyongesa
A Conversation..., A Contact by Tendai Rinos Mwanaka
A Dark Energy by Tendai Rinos Mwanaka
Keys in the River: New and Collected Stories by Tendai Rinos Mwanaka
How The Twins Grew Up/Makurire Akaita Mapatya by Milutin Djurickovic and Tendai Rinos Mwanaka
White Man Walking by John Eppel
The Big Noise and Other Noises by Christopher Kudyahakudadirwe
Tiny Human Protection Agency by Megan Landman
Ashes by Ken Weene and Umar O. Abdul
Notes From A Modern Chimurenga: Collected Struggle Stories by Tendai Rinos Mwanaka
Another Chance by Chinweike Ofodile
Pano Chalo/Frawn of the Great by Stephen Mpashi, translated by Austin Kaluba
Kumafulatsi by Wonder Guchu
The Policeman Also Dies and Other Plays by Solomon A. Awuzie
Fragmented Lives by Imali J Abala
In the Beyond by Talent Madhuku
Zororo Risina Zororo by Oscar Gwiriri
Sword of Vengeance by Olatubosun David
Finding A Way Home by Tendai Mwanaka
Your Epistle by Solomon A Awuzie

The Restless Run and Ruin of the Roaches and Rats by McLayode
The Reign of Terror by Ntando Gerald
Ibala Lyabwina Nama by Austin Kaluba
Daddy, Please Don't Kill Mama by Natisha Parsons
Pilate's Angels by Goodenough Mashego
Blue threads and other stories by Matthew Kunashe Chikono
The Sylvia Plath Effect by Abigail George
The Twins by Shakemore Dirani
I, Robert's Robot and other stories by Marvel Chukwudi Pephel
Conversation With My Mother by Wonder Guchu
Stranger In Her Own Skin by William Mpina

Soon to be released

https://facebook.com/MwanakaMediaAndPublishing/